SUGAR BEAR

SUGAR DADDIES #3

CHARITY PARKERSON

Punk & Sissy

--Warning: This book is intended for readers over the age of 18.

Copyright © 2018 Charity Parkerson
Editor: Vicky Reese

ISBN-13: 978-1-946099-35-8

INTRODUCTION

WHEN TWO MEN WITH ZERO INHIBITIONS START
A GAME OF TRUTH OR DARE, A LOVE AFFAIR
IS BORN.

Things with Jude started so harmless. One nice conversation, an offer to get drinks, and then nothing was innocent any longer. Hendrix has a past. One he strives to keep hidden. For that reason, and several others, he's always kept to himself. It isn't until he gets to know Jude that he lets himself live again, but not without fear. Hendrix never forgets Jude doesn't know him and wouldn't like him if he did.

Despite their almost twenty-year age difference, Hendrix is the best thing that's ever happened to Jude. He's smart, enjoys all the same interests, and is kinky as hell. On paper, they're perfect together. The reality is, Hendrix is hiding something. Jude won't stop until he uncovers the truth or destroys them trying.

When Hendrix's past slaps Jude in the face, he'll have to choose—accept what he's learned or lose the greatest man he's ever met.

I need to send a huge thank you to Randy from RLS images. First, for being my friend. Second, for fanning the creative flames for this book while trying to convince my husband to be on the cover. Love you.

ONE

THERE WAS STILL at least an hour until Hendrix's next gig. Since Maverick moved to the big leagues and now only fought on occasion, Hendrix had been forced to find new bet fighters to work with. No more often than Zeke and Maverick fought, Hendrix couldn't afford not to branch out, finding new ways to put his corner man experience to use. Most of the time, he wasn't forced to wait quite so long between the bouts he worked. Tonight, everything seemed out of whack. Not only did he have long intervals between matches, his leg was on fire. It ached. Pins and needles stabbed him from ankle to hip. The noise was also too much.

Sitting near the cage or down the hallway to the locker rooms was out of the question. Both areas were too packed. Fortunately, Luna Hotel, where matches were held, had several hallways leading away from the fight floor. Each passage led to elevators, taking patrons to the casino or their rooms. Luckily for Hendrix, they also had several alcoves with benches where people could relax while charging their devices.

Hendrix headed down the closest hall. He passed several benches where only one person sat. Since he had no desire to sit with a stranger, he kept moving, searching for an empty spot. He walked farther than his leg liked. Finally, a familiar face came into view. Jude Green sat alone, staring at an e-reader, and obviously lost in his head. Hendrix sat. He bit back a pained moan as he stretched his bad leg. After having every bone shattered in his left leg five years ago, nothing had been the same. Hendrix understood chronic pain in a way he wouldn't wish on anyone.

With the pressure easing and his muscles no longer screaming, Hendrix found himself staring at the screen of Jude's device. He caught himself smiling over his own ridiculousness. They didn't know each other except by name. In fact, he'd only spoken to Jude once, and Hendrix had been plastered at the time. Yet, Hendrix had walked way too far while grinding his teeth from the pain, just to sit next to him. The human condition was odd. Like everyone else, he was more concerned with his mental comfort than his physical needs. Not knowing Jude better than he did, he should've stopped long before now.

Before Hendrix realized what he was doing, his eyes swept from side to side, following along with the words of Jude's book. Jude's hand moved to the device, as if to swipe to the next page. He hesitated.

"Have you finished?"

Hendrix's gaze shot to Jude's face. He didn't look annoyed or amused. The man simply waited for Hendrix's answer. "Sorry," Hendrix mumbled, looking away.

"If I was bothered, I would've moved." Jude shifted closer, tilting the e-reader so Hendrix could see it better. "Have you finished?"

A small smile tugged at Hendrix's lips. "Don't worry over me. I've read that book already."

"Me too," Jude admitted, leaning back against the wall. "This is probably my fourth time."

"I didn't mean to disturb you." Hendrix didn't know why it troubled him that Jude had stopped reading to talk to him, but there it was.

Jude swiped to the next page. "You're not."

Still, Hendrix was determined to be quiet and leave the man in peace. With his back pressed to the wall, Hendrix tried closing his eyes and clearing his mind. Instead, Jude's scent captured his thoughts. There was something familiar and soothing about Jude's cologne. Hendrix sucked in a deep breath, letting the scent wash over him. He also smelled like spearmint. Hendrix peeked open one eye and tried to see if Jude had gum in his mouth. His gaze swept over the man. Jude took up too much space with his wide shoulders and massive biceps. Hendrix wanted to ask his age. His introverted nature stopped him. It was hard to guess, since Jude kept his head shaved bald, but there was quite a bit of gray mixed into the man's dark beard. There were laugh lines around his light-gray eyes as well. When he realized he was staring, Hendrix closed his eyes again. Damn. Jude smelled good. It was a comforting scent. Every muscle in his body relaxed.

"Jude." The bellow of Jude's name sent Hendrix's heart racing. His eyes shot open. Wyld West strolled their way, looking exactly like a man with a ridiculous name who owned the world. In truth, the guy probably only owned a quarter of it, but he still looked every bit as untamed as his name.

Jude closed the cover of his e-reader. "Fuck."

Hendrix smiled at the muttered curse.

"Wyld," Jude said, sounding less than welcoming. He didn't say anything else. Hendrix bit the inside of his cheek to keep from laughing. Jude hadn't made any attempt to welcome a conversation with the man.

That didn't appear to matter. Wyld's smile turned wicked. "I don't suppose you'd care to tell me who you're here to scout? That way, I can go ahead and scoop him out from underneath you and be done with this place."

Hendrix looked away, hoping to hide his eye roll.

Wyld's gaze swept Hendrix's way before focusing once more on Jude. "I know you're not here for this one. That leg makes him pretty much useless. No offense," Wyld added, as if those two words ever made anything less insulting.

"If you'll excuse me," Hendrix said, attempting to push to his feet and get away. He wanted no part of this.

Jude's massive arm shot out, stopping Hendrix from leaving. The man's gaze never wavered from Wyld. "Actually, you're interrupting our meeting."

Wyld focused on Hendrix for a half second before his gaze slid back Jude's way. "Interesting. We'll catch up later and you can tell me what you're planning." Without waiting for an agreement, Wyld strolled away. Even the man's personal assistant looked self-absorbed as they passed. Hendrix caught himself narrowing his eyes at the man. Loathing rose inside him.

"I've always hated that guy," Hendrix said more to himself.

Jude shrugged. "Everyone hates that guy. That's why everything he touches turns to gold. He doesn't care if anyone likes him, if he steps on toes, or makes a thousand enemies. That's what it takes to be as successful as he is."

"Hmmm," was all Hendrix could manage. Wyld had already ruined his mood, which was always only bleak at best. His eyes wouldn't move from the sight of Wyld making his way toward the fights. He'd met one too many men like Wyld in his life and been destroyed by the contact.

"May I ask you about your leg?" Jude asked, decimating what was left of Hendrix's already thin congeniality.

A growl rose in Hendrix's throat and sounded in his voice. "No." This time, he didn't let Jude stop him from leaving. Without a backward glance, he left Jude behind.

SOME PEOPLE WERE ALWAYS ANGRY. HENDRIX was one of those people. Jude didn't think he'd ever seen the man smile. Even though this was only the second time they'd spoken, Jude had seen the guy hundreds of times at various matches. Jude wasn't the type to pry into another man's misfortune. Nor did he normally find bitterness attractive, but as he watched Hendrix limp away, Jude caught himself watching Hendrix's ass. Damn. Tight and sexy.

The boy also possessed the clearest green eyes he'd ever seen. He wanted to call them emerald, but they were lighter than that. Hendrix was a unique beauty with his strawberry blond hair that leaned more toward the berry and plump lips that belonged on a woman. He was a reader too. That was an attribute Jude appreciated and usually showed a certain level of intelligence. Jude fought the urge to chase after Hendrix. The only thing stopping him was a clear twenty-year age difference.

Fuck it. Jude gathered his stuff and went after him. Between Hendrix's limp slowing him and Jude's long legs, he caught the boy in no time. He clasped his e-reader behind his back and matched

Hendrix's pace. "Have you read the second book in the series?"

Green irises flashed his way before staring straight ahead again. "No. I stopped at the first."

"Honestly, I almost did too. No one needs a ten-page description of every room a character enters or fifteen pages on what everyone wore. I've seen a blue couch. Just say it's blue."

The way Hendrix's cheek curved made Jude's breath catch. "I skipped those parts," Hendrix admitted with a chuckle. "After the fifth time someone stopped in front of a mirror and spent ten pages on the color of their own eyes, I learned to skim until they were past all that. Like you, I've seen brown eyes. It's okay to just say they're brown. That's not what turned me off though. It was the main character's unrealistic reactions to everything that happened to her. She was an intelligent woman, living in a harsh world where she had few options. That doesn't mean she would brush off a physical attack as if it never happened and start searching for ways it could benefit her. She came off as one dimensional and cold."

Jude nodded, getting lost in their conversation. "I'd like to say, after six books into the series, that part gets better. It doesn't."

A soft chuckle rumbled from Hendrix, forcing Jude to take a deep breath. He shouldn't be this interested in someone like Hendrix—caustic and too young. "Then why are you reading it for the fourth time?"

"The suspension of reality," Jude answered with a shrug. "I love the huge wolves and worlds covered in ice. The idea of surviving, even thriving, when all odds seem stacked against you."

Hendrix paused and faced Jude. His gaze moved over Jude's face. He opened his mouth as if to speak before obviously changing his mind. A sardonic smile touched the man's lips. Hendrix shook his head —like shaking away whatever thoughts he'd chosen not to share. "I have to get Detroit ready to get in the cage."

Disappointment washed over Jude. He felt like he'd missed something important. A moment he'd never get back. "It's been nice chatting with you."

Hendrix dipped his chin. "You too." He turned away and headed for the locker room. Jude watched him go, kicking himself for not making more of their time together. Before Jude had too much time to be disappointed, Hendrix stopped, and then back tracked. "I'm sorry I got defensive earlier and walked away."

"Think nothing of it," Jude said, fighting not to smile. It seemed Hendrix wasn't such a cold person after all. Just awkward.

"Maybe we could get coffee sometime and you can ask me whatever you like." Hendrix didn't meet his gaze as he made the offer, as if he expected to get shot down.

"What are you doing after Detroit's match?"

Hendrix's gaze collided with Jude's. "Nothing."

"Have a drink with me."

"Okay," Hendrix said before walking away without making any firm plans.

Jude bit back a chuckle. It seemed he'd have to hunt the man down to get that drink. Jude wasn't opposed. In fact, he was downright intrigued. Since Detroit had already let him know he wasn't interested in a sponsorship, maybe this new development meant the night wasn't a complete bust after all.

TWO

DETROIT WENT A FULL FIVE ROUNDS.
Hendrix earned his money, keeping the man
motivated to stay ahead. Detroit was shorter than his
opponent, making it harder to land blows. In the end,
Detroit pulled off the win by being only one strike
ahead. Hendrix tried not to show his relief. He
couldn't afford the loss. With bills to pay, winnings
were everything. Maybe next week would be the
week he stopped worrying over it. For now, he had
plans to get a drink. He never lost sight of Jude. Not
once all night. Asking the man to coffee had been an
impulsive move. One he didn't regret. Jude was
easily twenty years older than Hendrix, but it was
amazing how few things mattered when there was no
chance for a future.

The minute he'd cashed out and handed Detroit his winnings, Jude was there. His warm palm landed on the small of Hendrix's back. The heat seeped through Hendrix's shirt, warming his skin.

"Would you like to head upstairs to the Sudden Skies bar, or find someplace else?"

Hendrix glanced over, meeting the most beautiful gaze. Each time he saw Jude, Hendrix was struck anew by how gorgeous the man was. His mouth went dry. "I thought we'd head upstairs. Zander keeps a running tab for me here."

Something dark flashed in Jude's eyes. "I'm guessing that's thanks to Maverick."

Zander Kapra owned every single fight club on the West Coast. No one fought here without his permission. Hendrix had known the man his whole life, but if Jude needed to believe any running credit was thanks to Maverick, that worked for him. "Of course."

The pressure against the small of Hendrix's back increased. Jude steered him toward the closest elevator. "If you'd like to go somewhere else, that's fine, since I'm paying."

Hendrix fought an eye roll. "We're already here."

They stepped onto the elevator. Jude pressed the

button to take them to the upstairs bar. "True. Plus, they have rooms here."

Hendrix's mind went blank. He stared at the rows of buttons on the wall. He had nothing. As far as he knew, there was nothing wrong with his hearing. He blinked, trying to come to grips with the insinuation. Hendrix didn't know how to react. Since he'd lost use of his left leg, leaving him with a terrible limp, he didn't get hit on very often. Some guys overlooked it. Most did not.

"Should I talk about books and pretend I'm interested in only being friends?" Jude asked, pulling Hendrix from his internal freak out.

He turned his head and met Jude's gaze. The man's eyes were clear of all artifice. Hendrix preferred straightforward people. He would be the same. "I'm not friendship material."

Jude didn't laugh. He treated Hendrix's remark like a topic of serious discussion. "What makes someone friendship material?"

Hendrix shrugged. "Someone who calls on your birthday and texts to check on you." He felt somewhat put on the spot by the question when he couldn't think of a better answer. "I don't know. Someone who listens to your bullshit, even when they have their own bullshit, and don't feel like hearing it."

"I'm pretty sure you just described most people's mothers." Jude's deadpan claim left Hendrix wondering if he was joking.

Either way, he glanced away. Uncomfortable. This was the longest elevator ride in history. "What do you consider friendship material?" The elevator door slid open, freeing them. "Thank fuck," Hendrix muttered under his breath as he practically leapt from the small space.

Before Hendrix made it ten steps, Jude overcame him. He walked close enough that their arms brushed as he matched Hendrix's pace. "I don't have friends, nor do I want them," Jude said, taking Hendrix by surprise.

He glanced over. "Not judging here, but why?"

Jude shrugged. The gesture had Hendrix's gaze sweeping the man's sexy large shoulders before moving away. He didn't want to trip because he couldn't stop staring. "I've found most adult friendships very one sided. Your lives never seem to be in sync. If one of you is happy, the other is miserable. One of you is in a good place financially, the other is broke. And life always tends to revolve around the one who's in a bad place.

I'm mentally exhausted most of the time already without having to lift up someone else. Plus, I'm a bit of a homebody. If I want to keep growing my business, I have to scout new fighters to sponsor. But honestly, I'd rather be at home. What would you like to drink?" he asked as they reached the bar.

"Just a soda, I guess."

Jude eyed him as if searching for a problem. "We're at a bar, and you're having a soda? Jesus. You are old enough to drink, right? I know I've seen you in a bar before, drinking beer."

An evil smile touched Hendrix's lips. He spent a moment considering lying before he decided he couldn't be that mean. "Yes, I'm old enough to drink, but I'm driving."

After ordering their drinks and passing Hendrix's over, Jude focused on him. His intense gray eyes made Hendrix feel like the man could see all the way to his soul. "Now I have to know. How old are you?"

"Twenty-six."

"Jesus," Jude breathed, taking a swig of his beer and making Hendrix smile.

Hendrix glanced away and focused on the nearby dance floor to hide his humor. He lasted thirty seconds before he had to know. "How old are you?"

Jude didn't answer until Hendrix glanced his way, as if he wouldn't tell until he could read Hendrix's reaction. "Forty-three."

While carefully keeping his face clear of all emotion, Hendrix ran his gaze down Jude's body, taking in every inch. The man was huge and solid—like a brick wall. Wide shoulders, huge biceps, flat stomach, and goddamn... the man was sexy as fuck. Age meant nothing while running a business that sold clean foods and out-bench pressing most strongmen competitors. When he met Jude's gaze once more, Hendrix let the heat he felt show in his eyes. His mouth lifted in one corner. The smirk was out of his control. "Liar."

Jude looked away, but he wasn't quick enough to hide his smile. Hendrix sucked in a deep breath. He liked knowing he'd made Jude happy. He liked it a little too much. The awkward moment in the elevator was all but forgotten. Then Jude opened his mouth and ruined the moment.

Hendrix was amazing. He was forthright,

and his eyes always flashed with desire, whether he intended it to happen or not. Being blatantly honest was an underrated virtue in Jude's opinion. He loved it when someone said what was in their head, no filter or measuring each word. Hendrix made Jude want to know everything about him. That was the only excuse he had for continuing to push.

"I remember, back about five or six years ago, you were poised to take the lightweight championship. What happened? I had my own shit going on at the time and wasn't paying attention to fight gossip. But it seems like I remember hearing you were in some sort of accident."

Hendrix winced and glanced away. "I know I said you could ask me anything, but now I think I'd rather take a dare."

An unexpected chuckle escaped Jude. "What?"

The man's sexy gaze swung back Jude's way at the question. "You know, like truth or dare," he said, making a sweeping a gesture. "I take dare."

Humor owned him. Jude shook his head. "Are you serious?"

Hendrix nodded while taking a sip from his straw. "I'd rather do *anything* than tell that story."

Hendrix's confession made Jude realize his question had been worse than just the prying he suspected it to be. He was poking a painful memory in his attempt to get closer to Hendrix. That's not what he wanted. "Dance with me."

At the order, Hendrix's gaze swept the sea of swaying bodies. It was a slow song. Nothing too taxing. "I'll pass."

Jude wasn't backing down on this one. "You said you'd take a dare. I'm daring you to dance with me."

Hendrix shot him a defeated look as he set his drink on the bar. "Lead the way."

At the edge of the dance floor, Jude linked his fingers through Hendrix's. He tugged, leading the man through the throng to the center of the room. Once they were there, Hendrix surprised him by not backing down. He molded his body against Jude's and wrapped his arms around Jude's neck. Jude's arms locked around him. His heart skipped a beat. Before Jude knew it would happen, he buried his face in the crook of Hendrix's neck and inhaled. Hendrix even smelled out of his reach. This guy had no business with someone Jude's age. The knowledge didn't stop Jude from flattening his palms against Hendrix's back, doing his best to keep the man pressed as close as possible.

The need to say something—anything, overcame

him. "Since you took my dare, I probably owe you a turn."

Hendrix turned his head and met Jude's stare. In that moment, he'd never wanted anyone more than he did this guy who shouldn't be touching him. "Truth or dare?"

"Truth." Because Jude would do anything at the moment and that wasn't good.

"Why did you want to dance with me?"

Jude never considered lying. "I needed to know if you felt as good in my arms as I suspected you would."

Hendrix's gaze dropped to Jude's mouth. "Do I?"

"You're fucking with my head, for sure."

Hendrix's gaze never wavered from Jude's lips. "Kiss me."

Jude didn't need a second invitation. He dipped his chin. Hendrix met him halfway. Jude's hand automatically went to the back of Hendrix's head, holding him in place. An irrational fear that Hendrix would run overcame him. At first, Hendrix's kiss was tentative, as if unsure of what to expect. Then, his teeth sank into Jude's bottom lip. The world disappeared. What started as a need to taste Hendrix —with zero games, became a need to protect. Possessiveness mixed with desire as their tongues met, until all Jude could think was—*mine*. He'd never, ever been so immediately struck by anyone. Hendrix kissed like a man who made slow love. Jude found himself slowing as well, savoring, even as his body went up in flames. If they still swayed to the music, Jude couldn't say. His whole being was focused on their kiss. Hendrix was way smaller than him. At six-five, most people were shorter. In this case, not only did he have to lean over, Jude also easily engulfed the man's small frame in his embrace.

Jude moved from Hendrix's mouth to his ear. He pressed a light kiss against its shell. "It would be so easy for me to carry you out of here."

Hendrix shuddered in his arms. His grip tightened on Jude's shirt, pulling him closer. "You say that like it's a threat."

"We should get a room," Jude said while still placing light kisses against the man's ear.

"You don't know me."

"I'd like to." Jude wasn't backing down. If Hendrix said no, that would be the end of the discussion, but he hadn't. Not yet.

"Okay."

Jude was already leading Hendrix off the dance floor before the word died on Hendrix's lips. Anyone who cared to look would get an eyeful of Jude's erection, which—no doubt—couldn't be missed. He didn't give a shit. All Jude cared about was getting Hendrix alone before the man realized he should run. Jude didn't bother with guest services. He headed for the elevators, pulled his phone out in the lobby, and booked a room through the app. The moment he had a digital key, he had Hendrix inside the elevator, in his arms, and beneath his lips. His shirt loosened as Hendrix untucked it. Jude couldn't focus as Hendrix found his way underneath, stroking Jude's bare skin. The urge to fuck Hendrix right there nearly crippled Jude. He already had the man pinned against the wall and two handfuls of ass.

The door opened, saving Hendrix from a public embarrassment, but not from Jude. Jude swept the man down the hall. Inside the room, all bets were off. Jude chucked his phone aside, pulled his shirt up and over his head, and fell on Hendrix like a man possessed. He tossed the man onto the bed before covering Hendrix's body with his. Jude braced his weight on his forearms at the last moment, to keep from crushing Hendrix. The moment he had him pinned, and there was no chance of Hendrix escaping, something inside Jude calmed. His kiss softened. The way Hendrix stroked his back, lightly brushing his fingertips up and down his spine, had

Jude melting. He was under Hendrix's spell. Jude felt an overwhelming need to protect Hendrix. Please him. To always keep him safe.

Jude leaned away and kissed Hendrix's jaw. "You feel so small beneath me. I don't want to hurt you."

Hendrix's hold tightened. "Don't stop."

"I didn't say a damn word about stopping. Tell me what you like. I want to make you moan."

The tender touch was back. "Just go slow. My leg can't take much pressure."

Jude hadn't even considered Hendrix's leg, but he'd already decided to move slow. He wanted to savor every second. His lips moved to Hendrix's throat. He felt chill bumps rise on Hendrix's skin as he lightly kissed the man's throat. "Tell me where."

Hendrix's breath came out in a pant as he answered. "From just above the knee down."

Oh, yeah. He had this. Hendrix would only know pleasure on his watch. He eased Hendrix's shirt up, baring the man's chest and stomach for his kisses. Hendrix's body was small, tight, and perfect. Jude wanted to lick every inch. He'd never felt luckier. Hendrix shouldn't have looked twice at him. Jude would ensure the man never forgot him. As he moved down Hendrix's body, Jude stopped to kiss every place he could. Goosebumps coated Hendrix's skin, driving Jude insane. Hendrix wanted him too. The man couldn't hide it and didn't try. He writhed beneath Jude.

At the waistband of Hendrix's jeans, Jude didn't hesitate to pop the button and slide down the zipper. The instant he set the man's erection free, Jude had him in his mouth. He sucked even as he dragged Hendrix's pants down his thighs. Too late Jude realized he'd forgotten the man's shoes. With a growl, he crawled from the bed and tugged at Hendrix's clothes. At the last second, he remembered Hendrix's leg and gentled his motions. A soft chuckle came from the darkness, making Jude smile at the sound.

"What?"

"That growl," Hendrix answered. "You're every bit the bear."

Jude froze at the claim. "Did you just call me a bear?"

Hendrix laughed harder. Damn, there was something about the sound that broke down every barrier inside Jude. He couldn't stop soaking up Hendrix's happiness, letting it feed his. "It was a compliment."

Jude pulled out his wallet and dug out a condom.

He held it between his teeth as he stripped out of the remainder of his clothes. After ripping the condom open, Jude rolled it down his length. "Is that so?" he asked as he climbed onto the bed between Hendrix's thighs. Jude made a point of draping Hendrix's bad leg over one of his thighs, making sure he didn't hurt the man.

Hendrix didn't back down. "Yep."

Jude licked Hendrix's sternum, heading for the man's throat while swiping his crown across Hendrix's asshole. "What if I called you pup?" he asked against Hendrix's chin.

Hendrix sucked in an audible breath as Jude pushed his way inside an inch and retreated. "I'd survive it."

Jude was doing his damnedest to go slow. The only lubrication he had was the lubricant on the condom. He smeared as much of it as he could around the tight ring of muscles surrounding Hendrix's asshole, hoping not to hurt him. Sweat broke out across his brow. Jude didn't know how much longer he could stand not being inside Hendrix. Hendrix bit Jude's bottom lip, and Jude snapped. He shoved his way inside. A loud gasp escaped Hendrix. Jude held still. His heart raced, and his skin felt too tight. In that moment, he swore he'd never felt lust before now.

On his knees, with Hendrix's thighs draped over his, Jude controlled their pace. Hendrix was at his mercy. He refused to budge until Hendrix became restless, moving against him. After readjusting their position, Jude sat back on his heels and snagged a pillow. He shoved it beneath the small of Hendrix's back, ensuring the man's comfort before rocking inside him. Jude held Hendrix's hips. He slowly pumped inside the man, concentrating on every move. Jude could be methodical at times. It seemed, being with Hendrix was one of those times.

He calculated Hendrix's every reaction and matched it with his motions. Jude was mesmerized by the sight of Hendrix's cock bouncing and leaking on his stomach. He had to touch him. Stroke him. It was almost as if he watched everything through someone else's eyes. He was too turned on to think straight. His fingers encircled Hendrix's erection. The sound Hendrix made sent a wave of pleasure through Jude that nearly brought him to orgasm. He pulled and tugged. Hendrix's pleasure was his. Jude jacked Hendrix's cock as if trying for his own orgasm. Hendrix was perfection on Jude's dick. He was hot and tight, milking Jude. Jude was half crazed with need. Even though he'd started out slow and planned to stay that way, the sound of skin slapping skin let Jude know he'd failed. He needed release. At the same time, he never wanted the moment to stop.

"Damn, Hendrix. You're so goddamn sexy. Fuck. You feel good. Too good. I'm so close."

Hendrix's ragged breathing turned into a moan. "Come for me. I want it," Hendrix begged.

"You first," Jude demanded, increasing his pace. Hendrix's dick sawed in and out of Jude's hand. Hendrix whimpered and strained. His muscles tensed. Jude sucked in a breath as the man's asshole clamped down on his cock. He couldn't look away. A cry tore from Hendrix as hot cum hit him in the chest. The sight sent Jude over the edge.

"Hendrix." He couldn't stop pumping inside Hendrix, riding out every wave as he filled the condom. His thoughts and emotions were all over the place as he came down hard on top of Hendrix and claimed the man's mouth. Their tongues stroked. Everything felt right. Hendrix fought every bit as hard as Jude did to get closer. They took turns sucking on each other's bottom lip before going back for more.

There was a real possibility this was a one-time thing. In fact, there was a part of Jude that felt like maybe he'd been wrong for this. He was almost old enough to be Hendrix's dad. But no matter how many times that thought floated to the surface, it refused to take root, scaring him away. There was something about Hendrix. He made Jude want to learn his every secret. At the same time, it felt like they'd known each other forever, and Jude couldn't explain it. All he knew was, he wasn't finished. This one night wasn't enough. Hendrix didn't realize it yet, but he would. Jude planned to invade his life until the man begged him to go away.

THE BED FELT EMPTY. HENDRIX DIDN'T BOTHER reaching to check. He knew Jude was gone. Even though he'd known it would be this way—a one-night stand and nothing more—a shot of disappointment hit like a bullet to Hendrix's chest. It had been a long time since he'd let anyone touch him. Everything about the night had been against his better judgement. Still, he wasn't sorry.

Hendrix braced himself for the disappointment of being alone and opened his eyes. There was a note on the pillow beside his head. It was scratched out on the hotel notepad. *Before I left for work, I paid for an extra night, so you can sleep as long as you want. I dare you to call. 555-4259 –Jude.*

Hendrix hid his smile with the note as if someone would see him and judge him for his happiness. His cheeks heated. Fuck. It had been a damn long time since he'd let himself get carried away. Hendrix had never been much of a one-night stand type of guy. Doubly so since he'd ended up badly scarred and useless. But the way Jude had looked at him—Hendrix didn't think he could be blamed for being weak. His eyes fell closed as he thought about all the ways Jude had touched him. Hendrix's cock stirred. He already missed Jude's hands. Damn, the way Jude had looked at him while pushing his way inside. Hendrix had to take a breath.

He sat up and searched for his phone. His body ached in all the best ways. After programming Jude's number into his contact list, Hendrix stared down at Jude's name. It was too soon to call. The last thing he wanted was to seem desperate. But damned if desperation didn't own his ass in that moment. Hendrix fell back against the pillows and stared at the ceiling. His smile grew again. Heat rushed to his cheeks as he thought about calling Jude a bear. That damn growl though. It had been hot as hell.

Goosebumps rose on Hendrix's skin. His hand slid beneath the blankets. He palmed his cock.

The way Hendrix's name had sounded on Jude's lips as he came still rang inside Hendrix's head. His eyes slipped closed as he slid a second hand under the cover, massaging his balls as he stroked his erection. No one had ever handled him the way Jude had. If the man had done anything to protect Hendrix's leg from harm, Hendrix couldn't tell, but he'd not hurt at all. And, Jesus, the way Jude had kissed him, uncaring of the mess between their bodies—fucking hot as hell.

The memory of Jude stretching him wide had Hendrix leaking on his stomach. The sensation of Jude sucking on his bottom lip filled Hendrix's brain as he pumped at his cock. His hips rose, meeting each stroke. Hendrix shoved the covers down, and stared down the line of his body, watching his hand tug at his dick. He bit his bottom lip to hold in the cries. He pumped faster. That fucking sexy ass growl. Hendrix openly fucked his fist. He wanted to feel that sound around his cock. Hendrix squeezed and tugged. He was so close. Pressure beat at his crown. Light popped behind his eyes. Oxygen disappeared. Jets of cum soaked his stomach.

Hendrix fought to breathe through the waves of pleasure.

Hendrix's ragged breathing sounded loud in the quiet room. He couldn't move. His body spent. Still, Jude filled his head. Hendrix would have the man again. He had to. Nothing else made sense. It was like he'd known the man his whole life. If anyone asked, he couldn't explain why. It was like they fit. Hendrix needed more. He hadn't fit anywhere in a long fucking time. Jude had dared him to call. He would. Hendrix didn't think he had any other choice. Never seeing Jude Green again wasn't an option. He was hooked.

THREE

POWERHOUSE TRAINING WAS MORE PACKED than usual. It seemed like everyone in town had chosen Tuesday as their workout day. Hendrix was done with the crowd. With his duty to act as Zeke and Maverick's corner man while they sparred out of the way for the day, Hendrix ran through his daily workout. Even though he'd never compete again, Hendrix couldn't give up the routine that kept him in fighting shape. The months he'd been unable to work out while waiting for his leg to heal had been hell. Every day he'd hated himself a little more. Not only had Hendrix not liked the way he looked, the lack of exercise had fucked with his moods. Hendrix's mental stability was always a tightrope act without any extra pressure. The last thing he needed was to sit on his ass and let the dark cavern inside him swallow him whole.

He always saved the calf machine for last, because it hurt the most, and was always the biggest bitch to secure. There was only one calf machine in the entire place, and—for some reason—it was always the machine people chose to sit, stay, and surf the web on their phones. As usual, some guy sat on the machine, completely ignoring Hendrix's death stare. Hendrix's eyes fell closed as a warm palm slid across the small of his back. He knew without looking it was Jude. "What's the punishment for refusing a dare?"

Butterflies stirred in Hendrix's gut. He had to take a deep breath to control his racing heart. "If I remember childhood rules correctly, I believe you have to pay a forfeit," Hendrix said as he turned his head and locked gazes with Jude. Jesus. He was even sexier than usual in full workout gear and covered in sweat.

"Do I get to choose your punishment?"

Hendrix's eyebrows rose. "What makes you believe you're entitled?"

Jude leaned his forearms on the ab machine next to Hendrix. "You didn't call."

"Yet," Hendrix said, pointing out a hole in Jude's case against him. "I haven't called yet."

Jude shrugged. "That doesn't work for me. You've passed the three-day grace period."

Hendrix's smile was out of his control. "Is that a thing?"

Jude's eyes flashed with mischief. "Of course, it is. I didn't just make it up. Everyone knows, if someone doesn't call after three days, they're not interested."

Hendrix sat on the closest weight bench to stop himself from reaching out to touch Jude. Not to mention, his leg was killing him. "Obviously, not everyone has heard this theory of yours. As it happens, I planned to call tonight."

"Mhmmm," Jude said, sounding disbelieving. "Pay your forfeit with grace."

There was nothing Jude could ask that Hendrix wouldn't be willing to do, except never see him again. Hendrix couldn't do that. "Hit me with my punishment. I'd never want you to think I'd back down from a challenge."

"Have dinner with me tonight."

Hendrix crossed his arms over his chest before uncrossing them. He didn't want to look as desperate as he felt, but he was having a damn hard time not begging Jude to leave with him right then. "That's your price? Dinner? This doesn't sound like much of a penalty."

"Maybe." Jude's massive shoulders lifted in a shrug. "None the less, that's what I'm demanding to make us even."

Hendrix caught himself eyeing every inch of Jude. No doubt his hunger showed in his stare. "Since when do you work out here?"

Jude smirked. "I don't. It was fate. I spotted you through the window as I jogged past."

A chuckle escaped Hendrix. "And you just waltzed in. No membership. Didn't anyone try stopping you?"

"Would you?"

Damn. Hendrix loved Jude's confidence. "Where would you like to meet?"

Jude's triumphant smile was instant. "Nope. That's not how this is going to work. It's a real date. I pick you up. Take you out. You come home with me afterward."

Hendrix ran his tongue over his teeth, fighting back the huge grin growing inside him. He didn't speak again until he had it under control. "Fifteen-eleven Maple Way. Seven o'clock."

Jude put one ear bud in and straightened away

from the machine. "I'll be there. Be ready to go somewhere nice."

A groan almost escaped Hendrix, but he'd already agreed. "See you then."

With a wink, Jude started away, before turning back. "By the way, you look sexy as hell today." The man was gone before Hendrix recovered from the unexpected compliment enough to respond.

He needed to get this workout over with, so he could go home. His house was a mess, and it had been forever since he'd needed to dress nice for anything. For fuck's sake, the guy on the calf machine was still on his phone, hogging a machine he wasn't using. Hendrix wondered if he should skip it or pick a fight.

"What is it about you?"

Hendrix spun as the words were spoken close to his ear. His gaze collided with a set of whiskey colored eyes. "Wyld," Hendrix said, incapable of sounding welcoming. It crossed Hendrix's mind to ask what Wyld was doing there, but the guy probably owned the place. "What do you want?" he asked instead.

"You." Wyld leaned against the wall next to the weight bench and folded his arms in front of him, as if settling in for a chat.

"I'll pass." It wasn't that Wyld wasn't one of the sexiest men on the planet. He was. Hendrix just didn't like his type. The man's dark hair with the perfect amount of curl and runner's body equally had nothing to do with Hendrix's distaste with the man. Wyld had never been told no. He thought he was owed everything he wanted. Hendrix couldn't stomach it.

Wyld's eyes flashed with humor. "You didn't answer my question. What is it about you?"

"I don't know what you mean," Hendrix said, turning away from Wyld and going back to giving the dude on the calf machine the death stare.

Wyld closed the distance between them, invading Hendrix's space once more, slowly eyeing him from head to foot. "You have Jude's attention. At first, when he insinuated he was scouting you, I thought he was trying to throw me off the scent of his real prey. Now, after spotting him chatting with you a second time, I'm not so sure. So, what is it he sees in you? Are you back to training? Will we see the greatest comeback in MMA history?"

The longing that hit was almost tangible. It was also cruel. Hendrix stood, ready to run. He swallowed down the loss. The way he always did. "I have no idea what you're going on about."

"Hmm," Wyld hummed while staring at Hendrix in a way that had Hendrix shifting from foot to foot in discomfort. "If you don't wish to share what Jude sees, would you like to know what I see?" Wyld didn't wait for Hendrix's response. "You have so much hunger and talent inside you. It practically vibrates from your skin." He took a step forward until only inches separated them. Wyld stared down at him. Hendrix couldn't look away. The man's voice turned soft. Almost sultry. "I don't for one second think you'd fail if you chose to overcome everything you're letting hold you back."

Hendrix locked his jaw. His throat swelled. Wyld played a cruel game. He didn't stop.

"Don't shut me down yet. Hear me out. I can set you up with the best trainers and medical team money can buy. You give it your all, and if at the end of six months you still don't think you can do it, you can walk away. No strings or hard feelings."

An unexpected snort escaped Hendrix. "You think it only takes six months to make a champion? And no strings? Bullshit. Everything has strings."

Wyld's expression turned wickeder by the second. "I didn't hear a no."

"Because it's implied," Hendrix shot back. "Only a fool would think I could still compete in the MMA circuit with this leg. The best doctors couldn't put it all the way back together. Hell, I'm lucky I got to keep it." Although, most days that didn't feel like much of a win, especially the days when the pain kept him trapped in bed.

In an unexpected move, Wyld trailed his fingers down Hendrix's arm, tracing the line of his cut muscles. "Oh, sexy. I didn't say a damn word about MMA. You, my gorgeous warrior, are on your way to a lightweight boxing title."

Hendrix's mind blanked. "I'm sorry. What?"

"What's going on here?" Detroit said, slinging one arm over Hendrix's shoulders. "I already told you where you could stick your offer the other night. Are you trying to get Hendrix to plead your case now?"

Wyld's powerful gaze slid Detroit's way. Irritation flashed in his eyes. "What a gloriously over-blown sense of self-importance you have." He focused on Hendrix once more, leaving no doubt Detroit had been dismissed. "I'll find you Friday night at the fights. Think about my offer and let me know then."

Hendrix shook his head. "Save yourself a trip. The answer is no."

Wyld's smile was the most patronizing thing Hendrix had ever seen. "See you Friday."

"Damn, I hate that guy," Detroit muttered as Wyld walked away. Hendrix smiled over having the same conversation with Jude.

"Thank you for throwing yourself under the bus to save me." Hendrix rubbed Detroit's back.

Detroit didn't move away. His dark blue eyes flashed with good humor. The way they always did. "No worries. You know I don't like anyone and don't care if they think I'm conceited."

"You are conceited," Hendrix reminded him.

A bark of laughter escaped Detroit. He pressed a loud kiss to Hendrix's cheek and moved away. "Yeah, but I'm the lovable kind of full of myself that makes people want to take me home, spank me, and try to change me."

Truer words had never been spoken. Men and women tripped over themselves to be the one who broke Detroit. The man was sexy as sin and just nice enough to make people believe they could fix him. He was a heartbreaker.

Detroit walked backward and spread his arms wide. "I saved you. That means you owe me a kiss."

"Fuck you," Hendrix said with a laugh.

"We could arrange that too," Detroit said, tossing him a wink, and turning away.

Hendrix shook his head at the man's antics. Luckily, he was unaffected by Detroit's messy brown hair and that damn cleft in his chin. There weren't many people who could say that. Of course, most people didn't have a date with a sexy bear named Jude.

———

THE MOMENT JUDE PULLED INTO HENDRIX'S neighborhood, he was in love. It was like he'd stepped back in time, back when he'd known when the street lights came on it was time to go home. The streets were quiet and clean. Each yard seemed perfectly manicured with an overabundance of plants and flowers. The houses were smaller than his neighborhood, but perfect.

A smile pulled at his lips as he turned into Hendrix's driveway. His brown shingled house had a wraparound porch complete with rocking chairs and a porch swing. Jude caught himself taking a deep breath and trying to suck the perfect quiet life into his lungs as he climbed from his Range Rover. When he'd bought his house, in an upper-class neighborhood, he'd been achieving a dream. Now, he recognized how much happier he would've been here.

Jude noticed Hendrix's front door stood open as he climbed the porch stairs. A screen door kept out the bugs. He didn't see a doorbell, so he knocked on the screen's frame. Footsteps sounded on the wood floor. Hendrix's face came into view. The man's smile was everything. He waved Jude inside.

"Hey."

Rather than returning Hendrix's greeting right away, Jude chose to capture the man's lips the way he'd wanted to earlier at the gym. It was a quick, deep kiss that stole Jude's breath. "Hey," he said, lifting his head and brushing noses with Hendrix without thought. He straightened away. "I love this house," Jude said, hoping to hide his discomfort over showing his heart.

"Thank you." Hendrix rubbed his hands together in a nervous gesture that set Jude at ease. Considering they'd already slept together, they should've been more comfortable in each other's company. They were doing things backward—sex then dating. "Would you like a tour?"

"I'd love one," Jude said, meaning it.

Hendrix motioned toward a room to his left.

"There's only two bedrooms, but they're large rooms, and it's just me. Luckily, even though I was young when I was one fight away from having a title, I was smart, and bought a house rather than blowing my money." Jude stared at the light-yellow walls, shiny wood, and stainless-steel appliances of the kitchen as Hendrix spoke. "This place was built in 1908, so it takes a little upkeep, but I fell in love with it the first time I saw it. Plus, the neighborhood can't be beat."

Jude nodded. "I felt like I'd stepped back into my childhood the moment I turned onto your street." He walked from room to room, taking in the large, open rooms. The place smelled real—like wood and craftsmanship. He shook his head. "Seriously, this place is great."

Hendrix beamed with pride. "Thank you. I'd never really had a home before I bought this place. It's everything I wanted growing up, which is kind of sad, considering how small it is."

For one person, it wasn't small. Around eighteen hundred square feet combined with the small number of rooms made each room huge. Jude moved to inspect a large bookcase that took up one wall of the living room. He recognized most of the titles. "It's scary how alike our tastes are. I have a lot of these books at my house."

At the mention of his house, Hendrix looked away. "I imagine you're used to someplace much larger."

"I take up a lot of space," Jude joked, hoping to bring back Hendrix's smile. Hendrix's cheek curved a half second before he met Jude's stare once more. Jude kept talking. "Actually, when I bought my house, I planned to run my business from home. Even though I'd had a lot of success, I never expected clean eating to become such a huge business. Now, I'm in a giant house by myself while trying to keep up factories. I'd be much happier in a place like this." *With you*, Jude silently added, surprising himself.

"Leave it to Californians to run with a healthy diet and lead the world."

A snort escaped Jude at Hendrix's words. "True. Speaking of food, are you ready to go?" His gaze dropped to Hendrix's feet, taking in every inch of the man. His dark slacks and black Henley were perfect for the restaurant Jude had in mind. More than that, the man looked damn lickable. If Hendrix answered, Jude didn't hear. He found himself closing the distance between them. The man's full lips called to him. Jude recalled exactly how they'd tasted when he'd been buried inside Hendrix. "I'm taking you somewhere nice because you're worth it. But damn,

I'm fucking tempted to keep you here to myself," Jude said as he dipped his head and touched his lips to Hendrix's. For a moment, their lips clung. Once again, Jude found himself at Hendrix's mercy when the man lightly held his hips. He was always gentle, reminding Jude of his large size. "Give me your number," Jude demanded as he pulled away.

Hendrix blinked. "Okay."

Jude's possessiveness made him sound harsher than intended. "Now. Before you think to ignore me again."

A huge grin spread Hendrix's lips. "I wasn't ignoring you. Give me your phone." Jude dug out his phone and unlocked the device before handing it over. Hendrix held his bottom lip between his teeth as he held the phone and programmed his number. He was adorable in his concentration. Jude couldn't stop smiling while watching him. Hendrix glanced up and caught him staring. A light blush touched his cheeks. He could hear the laughter in the man's voice when he spoke. "What?"

Jude shook his head. "Nothing. It's just that you look..." Jude wasn't sure he wanted to finish.

Hendrix rolled his eyes. "I look what?"

"Sweet." Jude couldn't have controlled the admission if he tried.

Even the way Hendrix sucked in a hiss as he winced was adorable. "I'll have to work on that. Otherwise, you'll be disappointed when you realize nothing could be further from the truth."

"Mhmm, abuse me," Jude said, shuffling Hendrix toward the door.

"Pretty sure that's not what I said." The laughter in Hendrix's voice had Jude becoming more outrageous by the second.

"No? I definitely heard you planned to abuse me." He kissed the side of Hendrix's neck as he crowded the man's space while Hendrix fought to lock the door behind them. "Beat me, please? You hear me begging, right?"

Hendrix snorted. "We'll see."

Jude spun and headed for the SUV. "Yes. I'm going to get spanked later," he told a woman jogging by. She had her headphones in and there was no way she heard him, but he got the reaction he wanted. A burst of laughter sounded behind him. Jude fought the urge to rub his chest at the sound. Being with Hendrix did something to him. Whatever it was, he couldn't get enough.

Hendrix had been here before. Once. A long time ago. The restaurant wasn't really his scene. Not anymore. But, as he recalled, they had good food. The building was right on the ocean. Salt coated the air, and the view was amazing. Since they catered to the elite, the tables were set in such a way very few patrons could see each other. Dark tablecloths draped all the way to the floor. Short walls separated each table, giving the illusion of privacy. There wasn't a dress code since the super-rich would dress however the fuck they wanted. The right amount of money meant no rules. Still, most people dressed to impress.

A host, dressed in all white, led them to their table. Hendrix barely spared the man a glance. He was too aware of the man at his back. The one who was sweeping Hendrix off his feet with no input from Hendrix whatsoever. No matter the lectures Hendrix gave himself about not getting attached, he worried it was too late. Being with Jude was a tingle in his gut, an invasion of his every thought, and a lingering smile he couldn't shake. His brain screamed to pull back. The rest of Hendrix stood too close when they walked, brushed fingers with the man beneath the table, before finally sitting with no space between them. Jude draped his arm across the back of Hendrix's seat. Hendrix focused on the candle flickering on the table, hoping to hide the happiness overwhelming him.

"May I bring you something to drink?" Hendrix glanced up at the intrusion. The man's dark gaze was locked on Jude, freeing Hendrix from responding.

"Bring us a bottle of wine. I don't really care what as long as it's good."

Hendrix was pretty sure wait staff hated people like Jude and would likely give him the most expensive wine out of spite. But Hendrix had to stop himself from laughing. He waited until the guy walked away before calling Jude out. "You don't actually know a damn thing about wine, do you?"

Jude chuckled. The sound had Hendrix pressing a hand to his stomach. "I know that I like to drink. Not necessarily wine, but alcohol is alcohol, right?"

That wasn't true in the least, but Hendrix didn't care enough to argue. "I'm a vodka and beer drinker, myself."

A worried look passed over Jude's features. "I could send the wine back."

Hendrix found himself stroking Jude's leg, trying to ease his worry. "No. Like you said, alcohol is alcohol."

Still, Jude eyed him as if unsure. "Are you sure? I want you to be happy."

"I've been that since the minute you caught me reading over your shoulder." The admission was out there, hanging in the universe before Hendrix could call it back.

Jude's smile made any discomfort worthwhile. The man somehow managed to shift even closer. "Every passing second, I'm wishing a little more that I'd ordered in and kept you to myself."

"Would you like me to pour?"

Hendrix bit back a laugh. The server hadn't bothered saying which wine he'd brought, proving he knew Jude wouldn't care.

"Are you ready to order?" he asked once their glasses were full.

Hendrix flashed the poor guy a smile. No doubt he dealt with the worst of snobbery all night. He looked to be college age. Hendrix felt for him. He knew what it was like to be surrounded by people who thought the world owed them everything. "I'm sorry. I haven't looked at the menu yet. What's your favorite?"

The guy's relieved smile let Hendrix know he was right. No one was ever nice to the staff here.

Jude switched his gaze between Hendrix and the young guy taking their order. If he had to guess, Jude would say they were damn close to the same age. Yet, there was something about Hendrix's eyes that made him look older—like he'd seen too much. The more time Jude spent with Hendrix, the more he wanted. He was vaguely aware of Hendrix ordering. In truth, all he heard was his heart pounding in his ears.

Hendrix looked his way. "How about you? What would you like?"

Jude couldn't tear his gaze away from Hendrix. "Pick something for me."

"Okay." While Hendrix went back to chatting with their waiter, Jude cataloged everything about him. There was a scar at his hairline Jude hadn't noticed before now. No doubt the man had gotten it back when he'd been fighting. He wondered how Hendrix felt about never competing again. The man had been one match away from becoming the youngest MMA champion in history. Stories about his accident were vague. Mostly, they were speculation and rumors. Some people claimed he'd been in a wreck, but there was no police report to corroborate the story. Jude heard one person say Hendrix had been attacked by unknown assailants. Once again, there was nothing to back up the rumor. Jude wanted to try asking again. He loved Hendrix's smile too much to watch it fall, especially when knowing the real story wouldn't change the outcome. Hendrix would never fight again. Jude fucking hated that.

"I don't know what you like, so I hope that's okay," Hendrix said once they were alone.

"How mad will you be if I admit I wasn't listening? I was too busy staring at you."

Hendrix snorted. "You get what you get then."

"Can I have you?" Jude didn't know why he couldn't stop flirting.

A mischievous grin pulled at Hendrix's lips. "If you wanted me for dinner, then you definitely should've ordered in."

Jude's eyebrows rose. "What? You think I'm afraid of a public display?"

"Do you think I am?" Hendrix countered, but he didn't wait for Jude's answer. Instead, Hendrix's hand slid up his thigh beneath the table. "I'm here, paying my forfeit. Does that mean it's my turn to issue a challenge?"

"Seems legit," Jude said, trying to breathe through the lust Hendrix stirred with his hand.

"Truth or dare?" Hendrix kneaded Jude's growing erection through his pants as he asked the question.

"Since dares have been working for us, I'll stick with that theme."

A slow, wicked grin spread across Hendrix's face. "I dare you to keep a straight face."

That didn't sound good. Hendrix winked. He grabbed his napkin and slid beneath the table. Jude's gaze shot around the room, wondering how many people saw. Only two heads were turned his way. That was unfortunate in itself. Making things worse, they were faces he recognized—Zander and Maverick. The pair looked every bit as shocked as they should.

Hendrix tugged Jude's zipper down. Jude flattened his hands on the table and hung on. He tried damn hard to keep his features blank. If this was Hendrix's dare, Jude hated to think what his forfeit would be if he failed. Hendrix's tongue swiped Jude's crown. Jude swallowed—hard. He was so fucked. Hendrix being Hendrix meant the lightest of touches and the softest sucking he'd ever endured. Jude wondered if he'd tear off his skin. He was convinced he'd never experienced true lust before meeting Hendrix. The man knew exactly how to tease him into insanity.

Their waiter appeared at the edge of the table. "Your food should be out shortly. Would you like some more wine?"

A soft chuckle vibrated around his cock. Jude cleared his throat. "Um." Damn. Even to his ears Jude sounded strained. "I think we'll get our food to go. My date isn't feeling well." Hendrix took him down his throat as punishment for his lie. Jude bit the inside of his cheek, holding back his moan.

"Of course. I'll make sure everything gets boxed up for you." The man finally left him in peace. Jude's gaze swept the room one more time. Zander and Maverick were gone. No one else looked their way. Jude slipped one hand beneath the table and led Hendrix into a pace that guaranteed quick results. He couldn't do this all night. Hendrix's mouth felt too good. Desire made him half insane. He didn't care if he walked out of there with cum and saliva covering his clothes. Hendrix had him so close to the edge, Jude didn't care if the whole damn room knew what Hendrix was doing just out of sight. Nothing mattered but the suction on his dick and the ecstasy Hendrix promised.

Jude fought the urge to lift his hips. He kept his gaze locked on the table, seeing nothing. Hendrix had him trapped in his web. Jude couldn't imagine being anywhere else. Pressure built. Every muscle in Jude's body tensed. His entire being focused on the sensations Hendrix provided. An orgasm ripped through him, stealing his breath. Jude blinked, trying not to give himself away as the waves rocked him. Hendrix didn't stop. He licked, sucked, and swallowed. The vibrations on his over-sensitized nerve endings made Jude feel like Hendrix purred on his dick.

Hendrix fixed Jude's clothes while Jude sat in stunned silence, scared to as much as breathe. When Hendrix reappeared, Jude no longer cared about anything except the man who looked entirely too pleased with himself. Jude kissed him. The flavor of his cum on Hendrix's tongue only fucked with Jude's head even more. He wanted to keep this man. It was like there was something inside Jude, screaming this was the one he'd spent his whole life searching for.

"I'm impressed," Hendrix whispered against his lips. "If roles were reversed, there's no way I could've stayed quiet."

A laugh tumbled from deep in Jude's chest. Damn. He'd never been happier. "You're insane."

Hendrix pulled away. He eyed Jude, looking serious. "In a good way, I hope."

Jude's heart turned over in his chest. He needed Hendrix to understand how important he was. "In the best of ways," Jude said, matching Hendrix's tone. "Seriously, you're all I've thought about since the other night." Jude couldn't stop the confessions and he didn't care how he sounded, especially since Hendrix watched him as if hanging on every word. "I've driven everyone crazy this past week because I've managed to slip your name into every conversation. Thinking you wouldn't call was the worst sort of hell. I like you a lot more than I should."

A small smile curved Hendrix's lips. "How much is the proper amount? Because I have a feeling I like you way more than I'm supposed to for such a short period of time."

Jude's heart soared at Hendrix's confession. "If there's a rule book, I say we throw it out the window."

"Agreed," Hendrix said with zero hesitation. He dropped his voice to a whisper. "I'm damn glad you asked for our food to-go. You have no idea how turned on I am right now."

Evil overtook Jude. At the admission, he immediately made the situation worse by feeling up the man's erection underneath the table. "Good," Jude breathed, sucked into the moment. "I'd hate to think you were unaffected."

"They need to hurry with that damn food."

Jude pressed his lips to the shell of Hendrix's ear, speaking for him alone while teasing him by breathing into his ear. "Agreed. I fully intend to make you pay for that dare. You're in for a long night."

As Jude watched, goosebumps rose on Hendrix's skin. Satisfaction roared through him. The man never should've confessed to liking Jude too much. Now, Jude wouldn't let him get away. No matter how fast Hendrix ran when he realized exactly how intense Jude could be when he had his sights set on something.

JUDE'S HOUSE WAS GORGEOUS, AMAZING, AND located in one of the best zip codes around. Hendrix hated it. Of course, he didn't say as much. Not only did he not want to insult Jude, his dislike also had nothing to do with the house. It was the feeling the place gave him. The memories the house stirred. Standing there, surrounded by three stories of opulence, took Hendrix back to a time he never wanted to revisit. Still, he held his faked smile in place as Jude gave him the tour. Damn near every room had the same story—Jude never went in there. It was too much house for one man. Hendrix wondered if he'd hyperventilate. The sensation of suffocating grew with each passing second. This wasn't his life. Not anymore. He had to keep reminding himself of that fact. Otherwise, he'd drown.

"This seems a bit much for one person," Hendrix said, hoping he didn't sound as strained as he feared he did.

Jude nodded. "I've been feeling the burden of it for a while now. Like I said, when I bought the place, I thought I'd run my business from here. Maybe turn the bottom floor into office space and whatnot. Now, it's a lot of empty rooms. Several times I've thought about selling."

"What holds you back?"

After linking fingers with Hendrix, Jude steered him toward a set of French doors. He flipped a switch and the entire backyard lit. Hendrix's breath caught. "This," Jude said, leading him outside.

The moment the night air filled Hendrix's lungs, his discomfort fell away. Jude's backyard looked more like a secluded jungle—filled with flowers, trees and—best of all—a large pool. The water was surrounded by rocks, strategically placed to make it seem like a hidden gem. Hendrix eyed the stonework. Waterfalls poured into the pool. There were alcoves where people could relax beneath the waterfall or let the water rush over them. He was completely in love. "This is an awesome pool."

"I'm dying to know why you sounded so happy saying that."

Hendrix flashed Jude a smile. Before he'd lost his career, he had planned to build something similar in his backyard. Seeing it in Jude's was an amazing coincidence. "I love the water."

"Me too," Jude said. He moved closer. "Living in Southern California has it perks—like the awesome weather. When I'm home, I spend most my time out here, listening to the water, and relaxing." Hendrix's heart sped as Jude's palm slid across the small of his back. "Now that you're here, I wonder if I'll ever be able to enjoy it alone again without missing you." A happy sigh damn near sneaked out. That is, until Hendrix found himself over Jude's shoulder, and hanging mid-air. A laugh escaped him a half second before the water engulfed them. His nose burned as water rushed up it. He came up sputtering. Jude hauled Hendrix against him. The man's shirt molded to his massive chest, outlining every deep valley. Hendrix hung onto the man's wide shoulders. All humor fled at the heat in Jude's eyes. Hendrix blinked away the water running down his face.

"What are you doing for the rest of your life?"

A chuckle escaped Hendrix at the random question. "What?"

Jude's eyebrows rose. "Too much? Okay. What are you doing for the next two weeks?"

Hendrix didn't want to think. Everything about being with Jude had been impulsive before now, and he'd never been happier. He couldn't stop now. "Nothing I can't walk away from. Why?"

"I want to take you away."

The instant longing that hit Hendrix was almost crippling. "Okay."

Jude's smile was everything. "Seriously?"

Hendrix kissed Jude's shoulder as he held him closer. "Absolutely," he answered as he skimmed his lips across Jude's neck. "Whatever you want, it's yours."

"You should never give me that much power."

Hendrix worked on unbuttoning Jude's shirt. "I trust you." Plus, there was nothing Jude could do to Hendrix that was worse than what he'd already suffered in his life. He couldn't break the broken. Hendrix tried kissing every new place he bared. "Ask me," Hendrix begged once Jude's shirt hung open. "It's your turn." He went for Jude's belt.

Jude's words came out in a pant. "Truth or dare?"

"Truth."

Jude froze beneath Hendrix's touch. He gently cupped Hendrix's face, leaving him no other choice but to meet Jude's stare. His gaze moved over Hendrix's face, searching for something only he understood. "Tell me something no one else knows."

Hendrix's heart raced. Being with Jude was surreal. He made Hendrix feel transported to a dreamland. "I'm pretty sure I'm falling for you." Fear like Hendrix had never known stole his breath. There was no taking it back. Words once spoken and all that. It wasn't his intention to scare Jude away, but maybe he should be afraid. Hendrix had never been so immediately taken with anyone.

Jude's hold tightened on Hendrix. "Let's see if I can change that 'pretty sure' into a certainty." Before Jude's response sank in, Jude swept Hendrix beneath the waterfall to a hidden ledge. After setting Hendrix on the edge of the pool, he worked at stripping away Hendrix's pants. Hendrix struggled his way out of his shirt before lifting his hips and helping Jude bare the bottom half of his body. Everything in his pockets was most likely ruined. Not to mention, Hendrix had nothing else to wear. He didn't give a fuck about any of that because he was with Jude.

While waist deep in water, Jude fought his way out of his shirt. Hendrix heard something rip. Jude didn't flinch as he tossed it in the direction of Hendrix's sodden clothes. With his upper body free of the wet material, Jude didn't waste time. He tugged Hendrix's hips closer to the edge and swallowed Hendrix's erection.

A strangled cry escaped him as his over-sensitized crown scraped the roof of Jude's mouth. Jude sucking his cock was the sexiest picture Hendrix had ever seen. He couldn't look away from Jude's wide, darkly tanned shoulders. The man's beard tickled Hendrix's skin. Each breath he took came harder than the last. Jude was perfect. The sounds the man made left no doubt Jude loved what he was doing. It was too much. Yet, he needed more. Hendrix fought to get closer. He'd been turned on for too long. Hendrix was certain this would be the fastest orgasm in his life. He loved the sensation of Jude's tongue. The way he toyed with Hendrix's balls and teased his asshole. Hendrix's lungs stopped working as his entire being focused on one goal. For a moment, the world disappeared. Nothing existed except the pleasure slamming into him. Jude's name left his lips. Hendrix clung to the pool's edge, trying desperately to hang onto the moment. Life was never good to him without a catch. Hendrix was certain it was only a matter of time before he found the strings attached to this. For now, there was nothing but a happy glow. He'd take it. The good days were always few.

FOUR

THE FRIDAY NIGHT fights were packed. This would've been the last place on earth Jude wanted to be tonight if not for Hendrix. As much as Jude would've liked to have swept Hendrix away for two weeks of bliss the moment Hendrix agreed, the reality was they both couldn't leave until tomorrow. Between Jude needing to ensure everything would run smoothly in his absence and Detroit being unable to find a replacement corner man for tonight, they'd been stuck. With Detroit's match at an end, Jude searched the hallway outside the locker room for his man, more than ready to have Hendrix all to himself.

As Jude stared at a delicious ass that caught his eye, he knew he would recognize Hendrix's sexy backside anywhere he went. He almost laughed aloud when he realized he was headed in the man's direction before lifting his gaze to ensure it really was Hendrix. When Jude finally checked, his steps faltered. Hendrix wasn't alone. Wyld stood closer than Jude liked. Of course, in Jude's opinion, three hundred feet was too close. Something about the way they had their heads together, chatting, made the hair on the back of Jude's neck stand on end.

Wyld's gaze slid his way. Jude knew the exact moment he'd been spotted. Wyld straightened away, putting a little distance between Hendrix and himself. He said something Jude still wasn't close enough to hear. Rage boiled Jude's blood. Wyld had no business with his man. Jude had no doubts the dude was flirting. Everyone knew Wyld was a whore. Hendrix pushed from the wall and turned. His expression transformed the moment he spotted Jude. Jude swore even the man's eyes got brighter in his obvious happiness to see him. Jude's mood shifted. Wyld's presence was forgotten. Before Jude got the chance to say hello, Hendrix snagged the front of his shirt and reeled him in for a kiss. He scorched Jude with the way he sucked Jude's bottom lip with zero fucks to who saw them. For the first time, Jude understood this was real for Hendrix too. It wasn't just an obsession on his end. Hendrix saw them as something more. By the time Jude lifted his head, Wyld had disappeared.

Jude glanced around, ensuring the man really was gone. He focused on Hendrix again. "What did Wyld want?"

Hendrix shrugged. The way he eyed Jude made Jude wonder if he cared. "What does Wyld ever want?" His lips quirked, making Hendrix look downright naughty. "I think you should worry over what I want." He trailed his fingers down Jude's chest as he made the claim.

Jude took a deep breath through his nose. He had to remind himself they were in public. His body betrayed him, going hard. He already knew Hendrix wasn't above a public display. "Give me more than two weeks," Jude begged without thought. "We could leave right now."

Somehow, Hendrix's smile managed to get brighter. "I'm just waiting on Detroit so I can give him tonight's cut." His gaze slid down Jude's body, turning heated before meeting Jude's stare once more. "Then you can have whatever you want."

Jude melted, the way he always did in the face of Hendrix's open desire. When they were apart, Jude's mind betrayed him, whispering there was no way such a beautiful man could be his. Then, Hendrix would look at him exactly as he did now. In those moments, all doubt disappeared. His hand lifted. Without thought he brushed his knuckles along Hendrix's jaw. "Are you packed?"

Hendrix nodded. "Lightly, as ordered."

"You won't need much," Jude promised. "Not where we're going."

"And where is that again?"

Jude chuckled at Hendrix's thousandth attempt to pry that answer from him. "You'll see."

"I know. I know. It's a surprise."

The way Hendrix rolled his eyes had Jude biting the inside of his cheek. He couldn't wait to have this man alone. Jude invaded Hendrix's space and pressed his lips to the shell of the man's ear. "Detroit needs to hurry." Jude tugged Hendrix's hips forward, ensuring he didn't miss how turned on Jude was at just the thought of having him alone. "These past few days have been torture, waiting to sweep you away. All I've been able to think about is how sweet you taste and how hot you are on my dick."

"Hey guys," Detroit said, popping up out of nowhere.

Hendrix pulled away. His eyes looked unfocused and his cheeks were flushed. He didn't bother looking Detroit's way as he slapped an envelope against the guy's chest. "Gotta go." Without another word, he dragged Jude toward the door.

Jude tossed his best "What are you going to do" look Detroit's way before allowing himself to get towed away. He swallowed down his laughter. Since Hendrix swept him up like a tornado, he'd never been happier. Damn, the guy did wonders for a man's ego. There was nothing Jude wouldn't do for him in return.

"It's a yacht." Hendrix sounded horrified.

Jude eyed his favorite toy, trying to see the boat through Hendrix's eyes. It wasn't huge. There was enough room for them to spend two weeks holed up together without being under each other's feet. He'd stocked the kitchen and made sure the bed was made. Jude would make sure Hendrix enjoyed himself. "Just a small one. Two people can handle her."

Hendrix's eyebrows rose. "I don't know a damn thing about yachts."

A burble of laughter rose on Jude's throat. "You'll learn. Plus, we won't go out far. Just far enough so I can have you all to myself. I thought you liked the water."

"I fucking love the water. This is just beyond me."

Jude grabbed Hendrix's bag and waved him on board. "Nothing is beyond you." With a shake of his head, Hendrix climbed aboard. "We'll head out first thing in the morning. Tonight, you can adjust to the rocking of the boat."

Hendrix glanced over his shoulder at Jude. "Was that innuendo?"

"Possibly," Jude said with a wink.

Once inside, Hendrix stopped and turned in a circle. "Holy shit, Jude. This place is amazing." He met Jude's stare. "You realize you're completely out of my league, right?"

Hendrix's claim punched Jude in the chest. No one was out of Hendrix's league, especially him. He closed the distance between them and kissed Hendrix—hard. "Don't say shit like that." When he realized how intense he sounded, Jude took a step back. "Besides, this isn't mine alone. I share it with my brother, John. That's why I only asked for two weeks with you. He's got plans on the twenty-second to take her out. Otherwise, I might've asked you to sail away with me for good."

"A brother? Is he older or younger?" Hendrix claimed a seat by one of the portholes and gave Jude his full attention.

Jude tossed their bags on the couch and filled the spot beside them. "Older by eighteen months. He's always been an amazing salesman, so when I started Green's Fighter Fuel, I put him in charge of that department. I probably wouldn't have gotten off the ground if not for him."

Hendrix looked fascinated. "Did you fight a lot growing up or are you close? Oh, wait, is he your only sibling?"

A wave of longing overcame Jude at Hendrix's excitement. Hendrix was honestly interested in knowing everything about Jude—like he wanted to be a part of Jude's life. Jude felt the same.

"We fought always. Still do, in fact. He's my only sibling. What about you? Tell me about your childhood." A soft chuckle escaped Hendrix. The sound made Jude smile. He had to know. "What?"

Hendrix shook his head. "At the mention of childhood, this image popped in my mind of you as a child. I bet you were the tallest kid in class. You were adorable, weren't you?"

Jude snorted. "I wish. I was a short, fat kid. It wasn't until the summer before the eighth grade that

I shot up overnight. Still, I fought my weight. Bad genes," he said, explaining his battle. "Actually, that's how I got started with my business. I love to eat, but I swear I gain weight if I smell food, so I started searching for ways to eat better." Hendrix stared at him as if hanging on every word. A thought hit Jude. "How do you do that?"

A line appeared between Hendrix's eyebrows. "What?"

Jude waved in Hendrix's direction, searching for an explanation. "That. You always turn the conversation back to me. I bare my soul and it's not until later I realize you've told me nothing about you. I want to know you, Hendrix. Even if you think I won't like you afterward," he added quietly, because he needed Hendrix to know he couldn't be scared away.

Hendrix glanced away and stared out at the water. Jude almost wished he could take the words back. Almost. He didn't want to dig, but he also knew they'd never move forward if Hendrix couldn't let him in. Hendrix dropped his gaze to his lap and swiped his hands down his thighs. He pointed at his heavily scarred leg.

"This is courtesy of Gio Conti. You asked me about it that first night, and I didn't answer."

Jude's heart skipped a beat before slamming against the wall of his chest. He could hear his pulse pounding in his ears. Of all the confessions he expected, that wasn't one. Everyone knew Gio Conti. He'd been in charge of the West Coast before his death—Italian mafia. Jude didn't know what to say or how to react.

A sad smile touched Hendrix's lips, but he still didn't look Jude's way. "I was on track to be the youngest MMA champion in history. You know, I can't even claim I didn't know what I was getting into by signing on with Conti. All I cared about at the time was freedom. Money meant buying that house I love in a neighborhood where people feel safe." Hendrix continued staring at the water, as if he couldn't tell the story with anyone looking at him. "Everyone has this silent list inside their minds. A catalog of things they think they can live with... or without. It wasn't until Gio informed me I had to throw my title match that I realized you genuinely don't know what you can and can't do until you're faced with the choice." Finally, Hendrix's light-green gaze met Jude's stare. His mouth lifted in one corner in the most self-deprecating smile Jude had ever seen. "All I had to do was take one dive, and everything would've been different. Gio was dead two weeks later. If I'd just walked in that cage and gone down, in two weeks I would've been free." Hendrix shrugged and looked away again. "Instead, I refused and two weeks later, I was still in ICU fighting for life and limb, literally."

"Damn," Jude breathed. "And now Zander is in charge of the West Coast, and I'm sponsoring Maverick. I knew shit like that happened, but fuck."

Hendrix flashed him a genuine smile. "Nah. You're good. Zander isn't Gio. All that shit died with him. Plus, Zander loves Maverick. It's easy to see Zander as being the same as Gio since he was Gio's lover for almost twenty years and took over the business when he died, but think about what I just said—he was the man's lover for almost twenty years. Gio died five years ago, and Zander's only thirty-nine. Sometimes, we only see what people show us. In Zander's case, we see the billionaire who runs the West Coast bet fights. Not the child who landed in the clutches of a monster."

Jude watched Hendrix's lips move, saying things anyone with half a heart and brain should've figured out on their own, and it occurred to him. Hendrix was beautiful on the inside too. This terrible thing had happened to him, and still he empathized with Zander, seeing him as just another victim of Gio. He was, but Hendrix was right in thinking Jude had never thought about Zander only being a child back then.

"I think you're possibly the sexiest man I've ever met."

At Jude's statement, a huge grin spread across Hendrix's face before a snort escaped him. "Is that what you've been sitting there thinking about the whole time I've been talking?"

"I was paying attention, but pretty much, yeah," Jude admitted because he loved to see Hendrix smile. "You make it hard to think about anything else."

A blush touched Hendrix's cheeks and he glanced away. Jude wanted the man's sexy stare back. "Thank you."

Hendrix's face screwed up with confusion. "For?"

"Letting me in," Jude said, picking a place to start. "For coming here with me. Giving me a chance." Jude fought a blush as he realized how much of his heart was showing. He tried calling his natural desire to hide his feelings under control. If he was serious about Hendrix, and he was, he needed to show it. "Thank you for making me feel something for the first time in years."

"You should come here." The heat in Hendrix's stare as he made the demand had Jude coming to his feet without thought.

When Jude came to stand between Hendrix's knees, Hendrix tilted his chin up and met his gaze. Jude's mouth went dry. Hendrix's fingers curled around the waistband of Jude's shorts. While holding Jude's stare, he popped the button and slid Jude's zipper down. It was like Jude was paralyzed. Hendrix held him captivated.

"I don't think I've told you how incredibly sexy you are. You're all I think about anymore." He set Jude's erection free and dragged his thumb across Jude's slit, pulling a gasp from him. "I can't get enough. Do you know what I did the moment I woke up in that hotel room alone and surrounded by your scent?"

Jude was ensnared by the flush on Hendrix's cheeks. His touch. "What?"

Hendrix leaned in and brushed his lips lightly across Jude's crown. "I shoved my hand beneath the covers and palmed my dick."

Each breath Jude took came harder than the last. His cock leaked at the thought of Hendrix touching himself. "Do it again. Right now. Let me watch."

A wicked smile curved Hendrix's lips. He

shoved Jude's shorts down, underwear and all, baring the lower half of his body. Hendrix looked hungry. "For inspiration," Hendrix said as he leaned back in the chair and unbuttoned and unzipped his shorts. Jude couldn't look away as Hendrix set his erection free. The way Hendrix eyed Jude's body as he palmed his cock had pre-cum dripping from Jude's dick. No one had ever looked at Jude the way Hendrix did, as if there was no one sexier. Jude already knew Hendrix was irreplaceable. He couldn't go back to being treated like a passing fuck after being treated like a king by Hendrix.

Hendrix's lips parted on a pant as he massaged his cock. Jude pulled his shirt up and over his head before tossing it aside. He palmed his erection. Watching Hendrix was too hot. Hendrix flew to his feet and stripped, as if he couldn't stand anything touching his body. Once nude, Hendrix stole a kiss before reclaiming his seat. Jude's heart beat fast enough in his chest to make him feel winded. Being with Hendrix was a rush.

Hendrix licked Jude's cock before leaning back again. He held Jude's stare and stroked himself. A muscle in Jude's chest jumped. He fought the urge to pounce. Instead, he wrapped his fingers around his dick and tugged. Hendrix moaned as if it was his body Jude touched. As Jude looked on, Hendrix slid lower in his seat and spread his knees. He massaged his balls with one hand while jacking off with the other. Hendrix's abs flexed. Jude's mouth watered. He didn't know how much longer he could take this torment. Jude's crown was soaked and dripping. He was turned on beyond sanity. A sexy low moan escaped Hendrix as he pumped at his cock. Something inside Jude snapped. He pulled Hendrix to his feet. In an instant, he had Hendrix facedown and bent over the table. He dug through a drawer in the cabinet beside the table. Jude had never been more thankful for his brother's whoring when he found lube and condoms.

"Show me that sexy asshole," Jude growled as he rolled a condom on.

A whimper escaped Hendrix as he reached back and spread his ass cheeks wide. Jude's stomach cramped with need. He coated his fingers with lube and circled Hendrix's hole before sliding two fingers inside. He pumped, dragging more sexy sounds from Hendrix. His dick twitched. Jude palmed his cock and rubbed his crown against Hendrix's asshole, teasing himself. He couldn't look away as the tip of his dick disappeared inside Hendrix's ass. He pulled out. Hendrix whimpered again. Jude stroked his dick, squeezing at the root and dragging out the anticipation. He pushed inside again, watching as Hendrix's tight hole resisted him.

"Please?"

Jude's mind and body froze at the plea. He'd never make Hendrix beg. In a flash, Jude grabbed Hendrix's shoulder and slammed his way inside. A cry bounced off the walls of the boat. Jude couldn't stop. His hips rolled. He held Hendrix in place as he fucked the man's ass—hard. Hendrix's body tensed beneath him. Jude's eyes burned from his refusal to blink. He needed to memorize Hendrix's pleasure. Jude's name tore from Hendrix's throat as his asshole spasmed around Jude's cock, trying to suck him deeper. Oxygen became harder to get. Jude sucked air as he sawed in and out of Hendrix's ass. Every muscle in his body drew up tight. He held his breath. The pleasure dancing on his crown exploded into ecstasy. Loud gasps and whimpers filled the air as Jude tried dragging the moment out as long as possible. He didn't ever want to stop feeling like he did right now. When there was nothing left, he pressed his lips to Hendrix's spine. He brushed kisses along every spot he could reach. "You'll probably be the death of me," Jude admitted. He wasn't sure he'd last through two weeks of this.

A soft chuckle escaped Hendrix, making Jude smile. "You'll definitely need a professional cleaner in here by the end of two weeks."

Jude gathered Hendrix against his chest and straightened. "Let me show you the bed."

"Jesus." At the breathed curse, Jude stifled a laugh. Hendrix might be the death of him, but Jude didn't plan to go alone.

———

CURLED UP ON HIS SIDE, ON THE BED, AND IN Jude's arms, Hendrix was happier than he'd ever been. Their two weeks were coming to an end. Hendrix resented the passage of time. For almost two weeks, they'd done next to nothing except connect. He'd never felt closer to anyone, especially in such a short period of time. Jude was an ache in the center of Hendrix's chest. A longing. He'd rather sit with Jude in silence than scream anyone else's name in pleasure. Jude reached over him and turned the page in his book. Hendrix pretended to read. In truth, all he did was soak up Jude's touch. He was a glutton. His skin had been neglected of the sensation of human contact for too long. Hendrix couldn't think about going back to not having Jude holding him.

He shifted backward, snuggling tighter against Jude's chest. Jude closed his book and wrapped Hendrix in his arms. A happy sounding sigh escaped Hendrix before he could call it back. It was warm and perfect in Jude's embrace. Hendrix felt like the world had disappeared and couldn't touch him.

Jude nipped at the spot beneath his ear with a low sexy growl.

A chuckle slipped from Hendrix. "There's my bear."

"Pup," Jude said as he cupped Hendrix's jaw, holding Hendrix in place as he placed light kisses on the shell of his ear. Hendrix kept his eyes closed, savoring the sensation. "Tell me your thoughts."

Hendrix didn't know where to start. "I don't want to go home."

"Damn," Jude breathed, sounding as if Hendrix had hit the heart of his thoughts. "I can't even imagine going back to not holding you every night while I fall asleep."

"Truth or dare?" Hendrix couldn't contain the impulse for more after Jude's confession of feeling the same.

A low groan escaped Jude, making Hendrix smile. "Truth. I don't want to move from this spot to fulfill a dare."

Hendrix had already put it out there. He couldn't back down now. "Are you in love with me?" He cringed. Part of him wished he could take the question back. He didn't want to sound like a childish idiot. His nerves couldn't stand it. He didn't want to ruin things. "You don't have to answer that. I'll pick something different."

"I'm so in love with you," Jude said, cutting off Hendrix's panicked rambling. "It's crazy, I know. We haven't been together long. If anyone else told me they fell this fast, I'd call bullshit. But, there it is." He kissed Hendrix's ear again. His hold tightened. "I feel the way I feel, and I can't help it."

"Good, because I don't want to be in love by myself." In the face of going home and losing his spot beside Jude every night, Hendrix couldn't stop the confessions. "Since that first night together, I've made every crazy decision imaginable. I've never gone to bed with someone after one drink. It was a non-alcoholic drink at that. I've damn sure never gotten on my knees in the middle of a restaurant." He covered his eyes at the admission. Hendrix was horrified every time he thought about it, but he wouldn't take that night back for all the money in the world. "Not once have I told anyone I love them. It's like I don't know how to slow down with you."

"Don't," Jude said, sounding desperate. "This is working for us. Before you, I had my work and nothing else. By the time I achieved my dreams and slowed down, I looked around and thought I'd missed my chance at ever finding love. Then you came along, barreling me over like a hurricane. Now I don't want to slow down. I have a dare for you." Jude's voice turned sultry. His lips skimmed the shell of Hendrix's ear before moving to Hendrix's neck. Chill bumps rose as Jude's beard tickled his skin.

"Anything. It's yours." Even to his ears, Hendrix sounded breathless. Jude's mouth moved back to Hendrix ear. He whispered words he couldn't take back because Hendrix would never let him. Hendrix's eyes fell closed. Relief washed through him. He'd give this man the world.

Jude rolled Hendrix beneath him. His large frame kept Hendrix pinned while making him feel as if the ugliness of life could never touch him. With his eyes closed, Hendrix savored the way Jude's lips skimmed his throat before moving to his cheek. Then to the corner of his mouth. "Are you willing to take up the challenge?" Jude whispered. His lips brushed Hendrix's skin with each syllable.

"Yes."

Jude's mouth covered his. His tongue toyed with

Hendrix's. The moment was perfect. Hendrix almost believed it could stay that way.

HENDRIX STARED AT HIS SURROUNDINGS, soaking in the sight of the space he'd shared with Jude the past two weeks. So much had happened in the span of fourteen days. He'd never felt more blessed, or terrified. Hendrix didn't have the best track record for things going his way. The other shoe would drop. It always did. If there was any way he could stop the worst from happening this time, Hendrix would.

"Are you ready to go?"

A smile pulled at Hendrix's lips as Jude's arms encircled him from behind. "Are you in a hurry?"

Jude pulled away, looking guilty. He rubbed the back of his neck. "You probably won't want to hang around long once John gets here. I love him because he's my brother, but he can be a bit much."

"Ah," Hendrix said, the picture clearing. "You don't think he'll like me."

In a flash, Jude had Hendrix crushed against him. He placed several loud kisses all over Hendrix's face, pulling peals of laughter from Hendrix. Jude wouldn't let him get away. Instead, he kept Hendrix wrapped tight in his hold. "I know he'll like you, baby. You probably won't like him. John is very loud and obnoxious. That's what makes him so good at selling things. You'd think people would like someone straightforward and loyal, but no. I found out fast after I opened my business that people much preferred buying from someone over the top. He's good for my business but hard on the nerves."

"Family. What can you do?" Hendrix didn't know what else to say. He was out of his comfort zone on this one.

"Speaking of which, will I ever meet your family?" Jude asked, setting him away.

"I don't have one."

A bright smile sprang to Jude's lips. "Raised by wolves. I knew it."

Hendrix tried to smile. He couldn't force his lips into that sort of fakery. "Yes, I was. What time is John supposed to be here?" Even to his ears, he sounded dead.

A line appeared between Jude's eyebrows. "What—"

"Did I hear my name?"

Hendrix damn near jumped out of his skin at the bellowed question. He turned to find a larger and older version of Jude. The guy was massive—like a tough bull.

Hendrix found his face pressed against an unfamiliar chest. Thankfully, the hug was over as fast as it began.

"You must be Hendrix. Holy hell, you're way hotter than I expected. And, younger. Jesus. Are you old enough to drink yet?"

Hendrix opened his mouth to answer.

It seemed he was unneeded for their conversation. John kept talking. "Not that I'm judging though." He waved toward two people standing behind him who were definitely not old enough to drink. The dark-haired guy might've been right on the edge of twenty-one, but the blonde girl was probably only nineteen. "I met these two on one of those sugar daddy sites. You know, I pay their bills and they keep me happy. Most people are happy with one younger lover. I believe the more the merrier." John punctuated his statement with a boisterous laugh. The girl beamed, as if proud of her position, while the guy shifted from foot to foot, looking uncomfortable with so much of his private business being shared.

Jude was right. Hendrix was ready to go after only a few seconds in the man's company. He picked up his bag. Jude immediately relieved him of the burden. "Well, we—"

"Now don't rush off. Who knows, I might be able to strike a better deal than this guy," John said, lightly punching Jude in the gut.

Jude looked uncomfortable as fuck.

Hendrix was starting to get pissed. "I'm good with the brother I have."

John's smile brightened. "Oh, it's like that, huh? You got marriage in mind." He switched his gaze Jude's way. "Just make sure you get a prenup."

Jude and Hendrix exchanged a glance. Hendrix hoped like hell Jude wasn't taking this to heart. God knew Hendrix was. He had nothing to offer. John might be loud and obnoxious, but he was also saying what everyone would think. Thankfully, Jude took control. "We have to go."

"Yeah, yeah. I know. All work and no play, but that's what keeps us rich, and these two have expensive tastes."

Once again, Hendrix found his gaze sliding the pair's way. God, he hoped they made lots of money for this. He felt demeaned just standing in John's company.

The girl shed her shirt. "I need to change."

Like that, his sympathy was gone. "Nice to meet

you all," he said, stepping around them and quickly heading for the door. Hendrix wasn't prudish, but he'd known people who'd truly had to sell their bodies and souls to survive. These children were ridiculous and left him with a bad taste in his mouth.

"I tried to warn you," Jude said quietly behind him.

Hendrix flashed a bright smile over his shoulder. "It's okay. He's fine. I just figured we'd better get out of there before we're treated to a show we're not paying to see."

Jude overcame him at the passenger side door of his SUV. Hendrix found his back pressed against the vehicle while Jude eyed him. "You're really bothered, aren't you?"

For so many reasons. Too many to make Jude understand. Hendrix took a breath. "He thinks so little of those people, he didn't even introduce them by name. I guess when people stop being human and become a monetary exchange..." Hendrix didn't bother finishing. Jude hadn't seen the things he had. He didn't know how to express his distaste.

Jude nodded, looking more understanding than Hendrix expected. "I get where you're coming from. Don't worry. My guess is, he didn't think to introduce Michelle and Jonah by name because I've already met them. As I said, my brother can come off as obnoxious. In truth, he genuinely cares about those two. Although, judging by Jonah's expression, he might be sleeping alone tonight after making them look like a couple of whores."

Hendrix took another breath. Some of the tightness eased in his chest. He fought battles Jude didn't see, and Hendrix didn't want him to. "Maybe next time we see each other, it'll be different."

Jude winked. "Don't worry. It probably won't be until Christmas."

At the thought of spending Christmas with Jude and all the months in between, Hendrix's smile turned genuine. "I'm hanging so much mistletoe. You won't be able to escape me."

Jude unlocked the SUV. "Speaking of decorating the house, where are we headed? Yours or mine?"

Hendrix wanted to say his because he loved his tiny two-bedroom house in the perfect neighborhood. But he couldn't offer Jude more than what the man already had. "Yours, I guess." There was a way Hendrix could match Jude's status and not end up like Michelle and Jonah. Hendrix just wasn't sure he was strong enough to pull it off. There was only one way he'd ever find out. By calling Wyld.

FIVE

HIS LEG WAS on fire and he was dying. Hendrix couldn't go home to Jude like this. His eye was probably turning black from the punch he hadn't been able to avoid when his knee had given out earlier. There was no way he could explain that to Jude. One of his bad spells was coming. He'd been here too many times not to recognize the signs. His calf muscle was completely locked. He couldn't do anything but drag his leg along like dead weight.

Time passed as he stared inside his open freezer. He blinked, trying to remember why he was there. Oh, yeah. Ice. Pain owned his brain. He couldn't think. His phone buzzed. Hendrix glanced over at the device on the counter. Jude's name stared up at him. Hendrix's chest hurt. He wanted to answer and beg Jude to come make this better, but he was stupid. He'd done this to himself. From the first day he'd trained with the staff Wyld assigned him, Hendrix had known it wouldn't work. The pain had been too massive. Still, he'd powered through another three weeks of torture, hoping against hope he could be something other than the person who warmed Jude's bed. Hendrix was beyond proud of being with Jude. That was enough for him and would be for the rest of his life. But, would it be enough for Jude? Hendrix wanted the man to look at him with the same pride. Not gesture over his shoulder at him like John had Michelle and Jonah, introducing him with laughter in his voice.

Fuck. He knew it was mostly the pain screwing with his mood. Hendrix couldn't be this person in front of Jude—bitter. The freezer's motor fired to life, casting another waft of cold air in Hendrix's face. Ice. That's why he was standing there. While holding the edge of the freezer in one hand, Hendrix dug through the kitchen drawer for a hand towel with the other. He twisted. Fire burst to life in his leg. A scream tore from his lips. Darkness crowded his vision. The room spun, and Hendrix spent a moment wondering why the floor was getting closer before he thought nothing at all.

—————

Since returning home from their vacation together, Hendrix had stayed every night at Jude's. He'd thought they'd settled on that. Then Hendrix stopped showing up. The first night, he'd paced a hole in the floor, blown up Hendrix's phone, and gone by his house. The place had been completely dark. Plus, Hendrix's car wasn't there. The second night, he'd started questioning every word spoken between them, wondering if it had all been lies. Jude didn't wait for a third night to come. He hated to seem like a crazed stalker or worse—an obsessed old fool. But he was already at Powerhouse Training, and he couldn't shake the horrible feeling in his gut that Hendrix was dead in a ditch somewhere. Jude crossed the room, making his way toward Maverick. Since Hendrix worked the man's corner, he hoped if anyone had seen Hendrix, it would be him. Maverick glanced up from where Detroit checked the tape across his knuckles. He smiled when he caught sight of Jude moving his way.

"Hey. It's good to see you in a less compromising position."

Detroit's head snapped up at the comment. His gaze moved between Jude and Maverick.

Jude fought a blush. Fuck. He was too old to be getting caught with his dick out in a restaurant. "I have no clue what you mean," he said, leaving no room for doubt they wouldn't be talking about that.

"Okay." Maverick dragged out the word with a chuckle. Thankfully, Detroit didn't ask.

Jude rubbed the back of his neck, feeling awkward as fuck. He cast a glance around the mostly empty gym. "Um, listen. Have you seen Hendrix lately?"

Detroit and Maverick exchanged a glance, making Jude feel twice as stupid and like a desperate chump. Detroit gave one last tug on Maverick's tape and left them alone. He didn't look Jude's way.

Maverick waited until they were alone to meet Jude's stare. He came to his feet. "If I had to guess, I'd say he was having one of his bad spells."

"What do you mean?" Damn. He hated feeling out of the loop.

Maverick's chest expanded. He looked everywhere but at Jude, as if trying to decide how much he should say. Finally, his unique honey-colored gaze focused on Jude. "Look, I don't know how much you know about Hendrix's injuries."

"You mean his leg," Jude said, interrupting.

Maverick nodded. "Most days, Hendrix grits his teeth through a level-nine amount of pain that would cripple most people. Somehow, he manages. But there are other times when it gets to be too much. He disappears. We pretend we don't notice. Everything is cool when he comes back. He'll resurface. Just give him time," Maverick said, patting Jude's shoulder. "Sorry, man. I have a scheduled cage time I can't miss."

Jude nodded and turned to watch him go. Zander came through the door and Maverick changed directions, walking into his husband's arms rather than the cage. Their lips brushed. Jude tried to look away, but his eyes wouldn't budge. Quiet words were spoken between them, and Zander glanced his way. Jude headed for the door. He'd already looked like an idiot once today and gotten nowhere for his effort.

Before he made it ten steps, Zander cut him off. "You really like him, don't you?"

"I'm not a stalker," Jude said, immediately wishing he could bite off his tongue.

Zander's face lit. It was the first time in memory

he'd seen the man smile. Jude blinked. Happiness transformed Zander into someone almost human. "That's good, considering Hendrix's history with crazy and overbearing men." Jude blinked at the statement. He had so many questions. Zander kept talking, stealing his chance to ask. "Not that stalking is necessarily a bad thing. Some men love it. Anyhow, I digress. You're looking for Hendrix, right?"

Jude nodded. "Maverick said it wasn't unusual for him to disappear."

Something dark passed over Zander's features. "Disappear might not be the right term. More like, he fades away—incapable of moving or coping. You'll find him at home."

"I already checked there. His car wasn't there, and no one answered the door."

"He's there," Zander assured. "His car is in the garage out back, and he's in too bad of shape to answer, but trust me, he's there." Before Jude could thank him and walk away, Zander flattened his palm against Jude's chest, holding him in place. "I told you this because I think you're a good man who won't judge him. Don't prove me wrong." He held Jude's stare. Zander's ice-blue gaze turned hard. "You once were right to warn Maverick about me being dangerous. I am. Just not to the people I care about. Hendrix has had a hard enough life. Don't fuck him up even more." Without another word, Zander stepped around him and headed for the cage. His gigantic Russian guards followed on the man's heels, eyeing Jude as they passed.

Great. The last thing Jude needed in his life was mafia issues. He wondered sometimes over his sanity. When he'd offered to sponsor Maverick, he'd known he was offering to pay the way to the top for a man who was literally married to the mob. Jude hoped every day he wouldn't live to regret that move. Now, it seemed the man was also protective of Hendrix for some unknown reason. Goddamn it. It was frustrating as hell to be ass over teakettle in love with someone he wasn't sure he knew at all.

At Hendrix's house, Jude let nostalgia be his guide, and kicked the welcome mat aside. He smiled when he spotted the key underneath. This damn neighborhood. Hendrix could probably leave his door unlocked and no one would bother him. At the thought, Jude tried the knob. A snort escaped when the door swung wide. He moved the doormat back in place, hiding the key again before heading inside. The place felt empty. It was silent as death. He picked up his pace at the thought. Everyone expected Hendrix to disappear and obviously no one checked on him when he did. The man could die, and no one would know. Fuck. Hendrix needed better friends. He spotted Hendrix before he cleared the bedroom doorway. For a moment, he thought the guy was dead. He stared unblinking in Jude's direction. Only a twisted sheet covered the middle of his otherwise bare body. Jude rushed to his side. Hendrix winced when the bed moved beneath his weight as he leaned in to check for a pulse.

Hendrix's skin was cold to the touch, but he was obviously alive. "Damn, baby. You scared the hell out of me. Tell me what you need. How can I help?"

Hendrix's eyes were red-rimmed, as if he'd been crying. "Nothing." His voice sounded hoarse. "Just hurt. Have to ride it out. Didn't want to burden you."

Jude had never felt more helpless in his life. He glanced around. There was an open prescription bottle on the nightstand but nothing to drink. The blankets were on the floor along with Hendrix's clothes. He couldn't stand by and do nothing. That wasn't in his nature, especially when he cared. He fucking cared. Jude stood. First, he grabbed the blankets from the floor. Hendrix was obviously cold, but it was equally obvious he was incapable of moving to do anything about it. He tried covering him up.

Hendrix winced again. "Not my leg. It hurts for anything to touch it."

Jude nodded his understanding. He tucked the comforter around every inch of Hendrix except his face and leg. Next, he checked the meds. It took all his willpower to hide his reaction over the brand and dosage. That spoke volumes as to how severe Hendrix's injuries were. In this day and age, it was impossible to get good pain meds. The doctors obviously believed Hendrix needed them.

"This says every four to six hours. Do you know when you took it last?"

Pain shone bright in Hendrix's eyes as he stared at Jude, as if barely comprehending a word through its haze. "Um. Sometime yesterday, I think."

Jude couldn't imagine being in so much pain his body seized up while alone and incapable of getting help or helping himself. Hendrix deserved better. "Okay. I'll be right back." Jude headed for the kitchen. He spotted Hendrix's phone on the kitchen counter, trying to crawl away with unread messages. Jude powered it down. The place looked like Hendrix had been struck down in the middle of making an icepack. His belongings were haphazardly strewn throughout the room. The freezer door stood open. Jude grabbed two bottles of water from the fridge, kicked off his shoes, and made his way back to Hendrix. "I plan to do everything possible to get these meds in you without jostling your leg. Do you trust me?"

"Yes." Hendrix's teeth chattered on the answer, making Jude wonder if he was still freezing or if shock was setting in. That second one sent his adrenaline pumping. Could this kill Hendrix if left alone too long? When was the last time he'd had anything to drink or eat? Fuck. Should he go to the hospital? With his panic rising by the second, Jude grabbed a pill, twisted the cap off the water bottle and moved to Hendrix's head. "First, I'm going to put this pill in your mouth. Then, I'm going to lift your head so you can drink. Don't try to help me. Let me do all the work so you're not tensing at all. Understand?"

Hendrix gave him a jerky nod. No one was more surprised than Jude when his plan went off without a hitch. He refused to move away until Hendrix swallowed down half the bottle.

"I'll be back. Let me know if you want more to drink."

Jude rushed to the bathroom, shamelessly

snooping through the closet and cabinets until he found a washcloth and an electric blanket. He tucked the blanket under his arm while he wet the wash cloth with hot water. Hendrix silently watched his every move as Jude cleaned his face with the cloth.

"You should've called me," he said, trying his best not to sound like he was lecturing Hendrix. Nothing was worse than getting bitched at while hurting. "The moment the pain hit, you should've let me know. I would've been here. Better yet, you should've come straight to me before the worst hit."

Hendrix still didn't respond. Jude found an outlet and plugged in the blanket. He switched it to high before covering Hendrix's body the same as he'd done before, leaving the leg untouched.

"This isn't your responsibility," Hendrix whispered, sounding tired and weak. "You didn't sign on for this."

Jude's eyes fell closed at the statement. This was on him. He should've done a better job at making Hendrix understand—he truly loved him. Unsure where to start, Jude pressed his lips to Hendrix's forehead. For a moment, he stayed like that, hoping any connection at all would make Hendrix feel what Jude felt. His lips moved to Hendrix's temple. From there, to his cheek. When he reached the corner of Hendrix's mouth, he brushed a light kiss there, before finally leaning away. He held Hendrix's stare. "Not only are you my responsibility, but I've got bad news for you—I'm yours. Since I'm almost twenty years older than you, I have a feeling you'll get stuck taking care of me way more often than I'll get to care for you." A smile tugged at his lips. "I thought you already knew I want the job, Hendrix. Making sure you're safe, happy, and healthy is important to me. You matter to me. Please drink the rest of your water, so you don't get dehydrated. Then, get some sleep. I'll wake you up when it's time to take your medicine again. You don't have to worry about anything. I'm here now."

Hendrix's hand rose. His fingers stroked Jude's cheek. Jude's eyes fell closed. No one had ever gotten to him with the smallest touches the way Hendrix did. He turned his head and kissed Hendrix's palm.

"I thought you were a hallucination."

Jude's throat swelled at the confession. Hendrix was far enough gone he thought he was seeing things. What would've happened if he hadn't come? This couldn't happen again. "Go to sleep, baby. I've got you."

Jude waited until Hendrix drifted off to move

away. He needed a minute to clear his head. His anger ran deep. He couldn't believe people had known Hendrix suffered these setbacks and had left him to suffer through the spells alone for years. It wouldn't happen again. Jude's heart couldn't take it. Hendrix was his.

———

HENDRIX CAME AWAKE ON A START AS A SHARP pain threatened to tear him into pieces. His gaze shot around the room, landing on a sleeping Jude. Hendrix's heart slowed. Poor Jude. His large frame was too big for the kitchen chair he'd set at the edge of Hendrix's bed. Jude's neck was at an odd angle and his arms were crossed over his chest. Guilt ate at Hendrix. Jude shouldn't have to watch over him. Hendrix rolled to his side. A whimper escaped him. He bit his lip hard enough he tasted blood to keep the sound from happening again.

The second he dragged himself to the edge of the bed, Hendrix took another pill and sucked down the tepid water Jude had left for him. Jude slept on, looking like a papa bear keeping guard. Hendrix pushed to his feet, and hobbled to the bathroom, hoping he didn't puke from the pain. Once there, he managed to pee, wash his face and brush his teeth. By the time he was finished, Hendrix thought he might live another day. Leaving the bathroom, he almost knocked over the lamp while trying to stay upright. Jude flew to his feet as Hendrix fell across the bed. A scream tore from Hendrix's throat as every nerve in his leg came alive in simultaneous protest. It felt the same as having every nerve torn from its roots. He prayed for death. Today was better than yesterday, but still too horrible for his sanity.

"I've got you. Don't move again." Hendrix heard Jude as if his voice floated down a long tunnel. He thought he might've blacked out for a moment. One second, he was on the edge of tears. The next, he was tucked beneath the blankets again and staring at Jude. His features were sharp. Concern etched his every line. "Do I need to take you to the hospital?"

Hendrix shook his head. He lifted the edge of the blanket. "Don't sleep in the chair."

Jude didn't move. "I don't want to hurt you."

Hendrix scoffed. "You can't make it worse. I promise. Just hold me, please?"

At his plea, Jude eased in beside him. The moment he was tucked in next to him, Hendrix rolled his weight to his good leg and cuddled against Jude's huge chest. The man's arms swallowed him, making him feel small and protected. To his surprise, some of the pain eased.

"Thank god," he whispered against Jude. "You're like a miracle." The pain meds were kicking in.

Jude rubbed his back and lightly kissed his hair. "It makes me sad to think how your life has been if you think I'm a miracle."

Hendrix couldn't think straight. He couldn't guard his thoughts or tongue. "You're the only good thing that's ever happened to me. I'll miss you when you realize you're too good for someone like me." He snuggled as close as he could get. Jude was so warm and smelled like heaven. The way he stroked Hendrix's back had him floating on a cloud.

"I'd never leave you, baby. I don't know how to make you understand that. What do you think is wrong with you?" Jude's whispered questions fell softly against Hendrix's ear, soothing his way into the darkness.

"Empty shell," Hendrix slurred as he slipped away.

———

HENDRIX'S BODY WENT LIMP IN JUDE'S ARMS. IT was sudden. Everything inside Jude fell silent. The sound of Hendrix's rapid, labored breaths assaulted Jude's ears. He flew to his feet. Hendrix didn't budge. He checked Hendrix's pulse. Jude didn't need to be an expert to know it was too fast. Jude tried shaking Hendrix awake. Nothing. Fuck this. Jude scrambled for his cell phone and dialed 911. They answered on the second ring. His mind moved too fast to keep up. He rattled off the problem, but he didn't hear a thing. If asked, he couldn't remember what he'd said. All he knew was time dragged. Waiting for the ambulance seemed to take years rather than minutes. Not once did Hendrix regain consciousness.

Despite his shaking hands and frayed nerves, Jude followed the ambulance to the hospital and made it in one piece. Then the real waiting began. Luckily, they didn't force Jude to wait in the waiting room with everyone else. He was led to a small seating area down the hall. A Dr. Wayne spoke to him briefly, introducing himself as Hendrix's orthopedic specialist before disappearing to treat Hendrix. Jude couldn't stop pacing. He felt like he should call someone but didn't know who. Every instance where Hendrix had turned the conversation from himself came back to bite Jude in the ass now. Hendrix said he didn't have a family, but surely there was someone in his life. Jude's mind came up blank. He was useless in Hendrix's time of need.

A flash of white caught Jude's eye. He spun, catching sight of Dr. Wayne making his way down the hall. Jude met him halfway. "We've got him sedated," Dr. Wayne said, jumping right in. "Hendrix suffered what's called circulatory shock. It can happen when pain becomes so severe the body can no longer endure it. Luckily, you acted fast. Otherwise, the organs start to fail."

"Oh my god." Jude couldn't believe what he was hearing. "How could an old injury cause so much new pain and damage?"

Dr. Wayne shook his head, looking resigned. "Hendrix has been told many times not to push. I don't know what he's been doing, but he's reinjured himself."

Jude searched his mind. "As far as I know, he hasn't done anything. We just got back from vacation not too long ago, but we pretty much lounged around the whole time. Since then, I don't think he's done anything other than his usual routine."

Dr. Wayne nodded. "His power of attorney has been contacted. We'll go over Hendrix's options once he arrives."

Confusion owned Jude. "What do you mean? I'm here now, and I'm—"

"Here we go," Dr. Wayne said, interrupting him.

Jude looked over his shoulder. Zander headed their way with his large guards following close. Zander met his stare as he passed. His expression gave nothing away as he led the doctor out of earshot. Jude stood frozen in place. His feet refused to budge. When his brain finally came to terms with what his eyes showed him, he took a step in their direction, determined to be part of the discussion. It was Jude's job to care for Hendrix. Then Zander would tell him what the fuck was going on. Before he made it two steps, a large hand landed on Jude's shoulder, pulling him to a stop. Jude focused on a set of sweet brown eyes. That surprised Jude since they belonged to the largest of Zander's guards.

When the man spoke, his thick Russian accent did nothing to squelch the understanding in his tone. "Let Zander handle things. He didn't suffer countless concussions and broken bones keeping Hendrix safe to let anything happen to him now. Come sit with me."

Jude switched his gaze between the pair discussing Hendrix and the large guard who obviously didn't intend to let him get involved.

"Come," The man said, waving him toward a set of chairs. "Sit. I promise Zander will make Henny better."

At the odd name the man used for Hendrix, Jude looked closer at the man. "I don't understand. What are you people to Hendrix? Why would Zander have power of attorney?"

"I'm Pytor," he offered. "Sit. I'll answer what I can."

At the promise of answers, Jude cast one more look Zander's way before moving to the chair. As Pytor filled the seat beside him, Jude wondered if it would hold the man's weight. It didn't protest, but Pytor's expression made Jude think he also expected the thing to give. When nothing cracked, Pytor leaned his way and kept his voice low, as if not wanting to disturb anyone, even though there was no one nearby. "Zander will make everything right. Your man will be okay," Pytor said, nodding toward where Zander stood with the doctor.

Jude had never been more confused, angry, upset, and scared all at the same time in his life. "Why Zander? That makes zero sense to me." He knew Hendrix and Zander had some history, but he was seriously confused.

Pytor sighed. "I'm not surprised. Zander and

Henny are reminders of each other's pain. I'd be shocked to learn Henny talks about us at all. Nonetheless, at the end of the day, Zander still raised Henny. He'll move mountains to ensure he gets the best care."

Jude's mouth went dry as thoughts failed him. "What?"

Pytor nodded. "Yes. If a hard decision needs to be made, Zander will do what's best."

Jude stared at Zander. The doctor said something. They turned in unison to stare at Jude, and Jude knew Zander had just been informed times had changed. Jude pushed to his feet. "Zander doesn't have to take care of Hendrix anymore. That's my job now. We were married three weeks ago."

Without waiting to see Pytor's reaction, Jude moved to insert himself in the conversation about his husband's care. Maybe Zander had been in charge. But now, he wouldn't be making any decisions without Jude.

When he reached Zander's side, Jude set his hand on Zander's shoulder. In the face of Hendrix's story about Gio taking Zander as a lover when Zander had still been a child, and the revelation that Zander had raised Hendrix, Jude was willing to give a little. But still, Hendrix belonged to him now. No decisions would be made without his input. "What are we doing?"

Zander gave the doctor a sharp nod, and Dr. Wayne laid out a plan to reconstruct Hendrix's leg. Jude nodded. There'd been some advancement in medicine since Hendrix's injury. This was the best option.

"But," Dr. Wayne said, looking dire. "There's a possibility we'll get in there and find the damage is too extensive."

"What then?"

"They'll have to amputate," Zander said, dealing the blow.

Jude wondered if he'd ever breathe properly again. He knew there was no other choice. Hendrix couldn't go on like this. Still, how would Hendrix feel? What choice would he want Jude to make?

Unexpectedly, Zander rubbed his back. "He's suffering," Zander said, pointing out what Jude already knew.

Jude nodded. "I know. There's no other choice."

With permission given, Dr. Wayne motioned toward Hendrix's room. "Things will move quickly. If you'd like to see him, now is your chance. He's sedated, but you never know what he can hear."

"I'll let you go alone," Zander said, showing amazing class.

Jude shook his head. "Come. Like the doc says, you never know."

With a nod from Zander, they headed in. At the first sight of Hendrix, Jude's knees almost gave out. A machine breathed for him. There were so many tubes and lights, Jude didn't know where to look. Jude didn't hesitate to lean in to kiss Hendrix's cheek.

"No matter what, I'm here, baby. You'd better fight to stay with me."

He hated this. Jude couldn't breathe. Every breath came harder than the last. Hyperventilating looked like a real possibility. When he'd married Hendrix, he'd pictured years and years together. Now, after just three weeks' time, he could lose everything. Jude pressed his forehead to Hendrix's shoulder and breathed in his scent. "Did I do this? Is this my fault somehow? We spent two weeks out on the water. Was that too much?" He hated himself for turning to Zander, but he knew the man would be honest with him.

"This isn't on you," Zander said quietly. "Just like me, Gio will forever be in Henny's head." Jude wished people would stop talking to him like he knew what the fuck was going on—like Hendrix had told him a goddamn thing. Zander kept talking, as if Jude wasn't ready to snap. "When Wyld made his proposition, Henny saw a way to offer you something other than a broken body and soul."

Jude straightened and turned Zander's way. "What proposition?" Even Jude heard the deadly growl in his tone.

"To rekindle Henny's career," Zander answered, as if Jude didn't have murder in his eyes.

"That motherfucker. There's nothing wrong with Hendrix. He doesn't need Wyld's goddamn promises of fame, especially to make me happy. I was already fucking happy."

Zander's eyebrows rose. "I'm aware, but if you plan to dedicate your life to a fucked-up man, get ready to endure some fucked up reasoning. Maverick does it every day for me. You'll have to dig deep for Henny."

Zander kept talking, but Jude had murder on the brain. Wyld had done this. He'd put Hendrix in the hospital just the same as if he'd taken a baseball bat to Hendrix's leg.

A dark-haired nurse and a blond nurse came through the door. "It's time to go."

Jude nodded. He gave Hendrix another kiss and

stepped out of the way. "How long will the surgery take?"

"A few hours, at least," the blond nurse answered.

A few hours would work. That gave him enough time to kill Wyld and be back in time for the anesthesia to wear off. Luckily, he knew exactly where the bastard spent all his time. Once Wyld was dead, someone would give him some goddamn answers. He was tired of being in the dark.

SIX

JUDE FOUGHT the urge to put his foot through the front door of the Den of Payne like he was raiding the place for drugs. Instead, he rang the bell. A man with mismatched eyes answered. He eyed Jude from head to foot. His expression gave nothing away.

"Are you lost?"

"No. I'm looking for someone." Even Jude heard the dangerous growl to his voice.

Mismatched didn't bite. "That's too bad. We cater to the lost. Is this someone your spouse?"

"No."

"Did they fuck with your spouse?"

Jude's temper didn't have time for this. "I'm looking for Wyld."

The guy's eyebrows rose. "It's against policy for me to breach a customer's privacy. However, I can offer you a tour, if you're interested in membership. If you happen to see someone you know along the way, I can't stop you from there."

Jude took several breaths. This guy was helping how he could. "In that case, I'd love to hear about your membership options."

The blond took a step back. "Welcome to the Den of Payne. I'm Payne."

Jude stepped inside. "Jude," he mumbled as he passed.

"Nice to meet you, Jude. Humor me while I show you around. What's your kink?"

He gave Payne the side eye. "Do we have to do this?"

Payne clasped his hands behind his back. The move drew attention to his massive chest. "If you're bent on murdering a billionaire inside my club, and ruining me, then yes. The least you can do is give the illusion you're interested in my services."

He thought about Hendrix as he scanned the room. "It seems I have a thing for much younger men," Jude muttered. There was nothing conspicuous about the place up to that point. It kind of looked like a doctor's office. Of course, given the time of day, probably only the dirtiest of perverts were hanging out in the back where no one could see. Wyld was definitely there somewhere.

"How much younger?" Payne asked as he led the way to a closed door. "Everything we do here is legal and consensual."

Jude shot him a dirty look. "You asked. I answered. My husband is seventeen years younger than me, but I'd never touch a minor. Get on with your tour."

"Oh, you're married. Good. We have a ton of fun activities for couples."

"I'd ask if you get throttled often, but I get the feeling you get off on that."

Payne flashed him a wicked smile. For the first time, Jude really looked at him. He was possibly the most sexual person Jude had ever set eyes on. Payne looked like a man who knew how to please. It dripped from his heated stares. "I get off on everything. Now, through here, we have a voyeur's dream. If you like to watch, you'll never get bored."

That was only funny because the first thing Jude's gaze found was a red settee. Wyld filled the piece. A dark-haired guy kissed Wyld's neck while his hand moved inside Wyld's open pants. Wyld couldn't have looked more bored if he tried. Jude was about to give him all the excitement he could handle. "Excuse me," Jude said unnecessarily since Payne seemed to have melted away when he wasn't looking. Jude's long stride ate up the floor. He passed a guy in some sort of circle jerk. Jude never looked his way. Wyld's gaze locked on Jude. If he was surprised or curious, he didn't show it. Instead, he continued sitting still, as if waiting for the guy fondling him to realize he wasn't interested.

Jude didn't slow. Wyld's eyebrows rose a half second before Jude ripped him from his toy's embrace. "We have business," Jude barked as he dragged Wyld from the couch.

"Damn." Wyld's dry tone didn't match his circumstances. "If you desire my company, you're in luck. I'm free."

While keeping a tight grip on Wyld's collar, Jude scanned the room. His gaze landed on a lit exit sign. Jude headed for the door, hauling Wyld along in his wake. The moment the sun hit his face, Jude slung Wyld out the door, sending him scrambling to stay upright.

Once he had his balance, Wyld turned and straightened his clothes. "I like the rough stuff as much as the next guy, but—"

Jude slammed his fist in Wyld's left eye. "You motherfucker."

Wyld's head snapped back. He sat down on a nearby metal staircase. The man cupped his eye. "Well, I probably had that coming. Just not from you, I don't think."

Wyld's calm cut through Jude's temper. He shook out his fist. "That's from Hendrix. He'd deliver it himself but he's a little too busy possibly getting his leg sawed off at the moment, thanks to you."

Wyld dropped his hand and squinted up at Jude. His eye was already swelling, and a cut flowed freely. "Wow. That's... what?"

Jude nodded, half out of his head. "He hasn't competed in years, because he can't. Thanks to you dragging him back in, he's reinjured his leg, sending him into circulatory shock. They might have to amputate."

The way Wyld blinked made Jude wonder if the guy was too high to have even felt his punch.

Jude growled and scrubbed his hands over his head. "Fuck it. Never mind. I see I wasted my time coming here. No one can even beat a sense of humanity into you. You're a waste of space." Jude was so fucking angry and scared and even angrier because he was scared, he didn't know where to go with it.

"All good points," Wyld said, still sounding entirely too reasonable for a man who'd just been punched in the face. "Except the part about me dragging him back. I offered. Hendrix turned me down. Then, he married you, and your brother made it clear he was no more than arm candy, living off your fortune. That's what dragged Hendrix back in. So, really, maybe you should hit him next."

The remark hit Jude harder than an actual punch. Jude walked away, leaving Wyld behind without a word. He'd done this. When John had joked about Hendrix finding a sugar daddy, he'd seen Hendrix's face. Instead of doing everything in his power to reassure Hendrix, he'd assumed Hendrix could feel him and know this was love. He'd failed Hendrix. Failed their marriage in the most basic way by leaving Hendrix isolated in his fears. It wouldn't happen again.

WYLD'S HEAD POUNDED. HE HELD IT BETWEEN his hands, hoping to massage the pain away. The alcohol and pills he'd mixed earlier stopped his rapidly swelling eye from hurting, but he hadn't drunk enough to fight off the after effects of his high. Damn. It had been a long time since anyone hit him in the face. His respect for every fighter he knew doubled. This wasn't fun.

"Sir, do you need help?"

At the question, Wyld's head shot up. He looked into the face of an angel. Short blond hair that curled in the sexiest way. Gorgeous soft brown eyes. Youth poured from the guy's slight frame. "Hello, Angel. I'm quite good."

The guy smiled. He had dimples. Of course he did. Didn't all angels? "I prefer Micah. You don't look quite good. You're bleeding."

"Micah," Wyld repeated. "The angel of miracles. I'm Wyld."

"I'd say more likely feral, but you're still bleeding."

A chuckle escaped Wyld at the boy's observation. "Possibly, but in this case, my name is Wyld."

Micah's smile kicked up a notch. "It's fitting."

Wyld pushed to his feet. "So, Micah, angel of miracles, do you usually troll the alleys behind hardcore sex clubs?" Wyld swayed on his feet, stealing the power from his building lecture.

Micah reached out to steady him. The second the boy's hand touched Wyld's arm, Wyld was transfixed. His gaze wouldn't budge from Micah's face. He was beautiful perfection. "Actually, yes. I deliver food to the homeless in the area once a week."

Oh, he was too much. Wyld wanted to lick him just to taste the innocence. "That's sweet. How are you not dead yet?"

"I'm not the one bleeding," Micah pointed out. He didn't sound the least bit insulted. His gaze moved over Wyld's face. "Do you need a ride to the hospital?"

Seriously, how was this child not dead, offering rides to strangers? Still, it was an excuse to stay in his company. "Actually, I believe I do."

Micah's expression turned worried. He moved closer. "What hurts? Come here, lean your weight on me. I'll help you to the car."

Wyld didn't hesitate to drape his arm over Micah's shoulders. Damn, he even smelled sweet. Wyld couldn't let the boy worry. "I do need a ride, but I'm not that badly injured. It seems my friend is in the middle of a life-saving surgery, and guilt says I should be there."

Micah stroked Wyld's stomach. "It's okay,

sweetie. You can keep your pride. Let me find Detroit and I'll get you to the hospital."

Wyld's brain stuttered. He nearly groaned aloud. Detroit wasn't that common of a name. "You don't mean Detroit Amherst, do you?"

Micah blinked. "Yes. How did you know?"

Because life hated him. "It's a small world. So, is Detroit your boyfriend?" He felt old as fuck asking that.

An adorable bark of laughter escaped Micah. "No. We've been best friends since I was a freshman in high school."

"You mean you're not still in high school," Wyld muttered.

Micah ignored him. "Of course, Detroit was two years ahead of me. I expected him to drop me when he graduated, since he's him and I'm me, but he didn't. We've stayed friends through it all. He helps me deliver the food."

"What do you mean you're you and he's him?"

Another sweet laugh caressed Wyld's ears. "If you know him, then you can figure it out. He's athletic and sexy. I'm just me."

He was fucking adorable and corruptible and Wyld was *so* going to hell. "Would you like to give me your social security number while you're at it?"

Wyld asked, because seriously he had no idea how this kid had lived so long being this goddamn innocent.

"What's that supposed to mean?" Micah asked, sounding annoyed for the first time.

Wyld felt something he hadn't in a long damn time—regret. Protective. "You should never expose your heart like that, babe. There are too many men out there who'd love to have that kind of power over you." He stopped, forcing Micah to stop too. The boy's concerned gaze shot his way. Wyld held his stare. "I know Detroit, and you're right. You're you and he's him, and you're so much better than he'll ever be. If I can say that after five minutes in your company, then know you should never compare yourself to him again as the standard."

"How hard did you say you hit your head?"

At Micah's question, Wyld started moving again. "Apparently pretty fucking hard." If there was anyone less deserving of giving a lecture, Wyld had never met him.

Micah helped Wyld hobble from the alley. They met Detroit on the sidewalk. His gaze moved between them.

"No," Detroit said, sounding firm. He pointed

toward the alley. "Put it back. This one is rabid and will definitely give you fleas."

"But he's bleeding," Micah pouted, sounding adorable.

That seemed to give Detroit pause. He focused on Wyld. "Why are you bleeding?"

Wyld held the man's stare while keeping his face blank. "You were walking past, and I was blown over by your gigantic ego."

Micah laughed. "I like him. I'm keeping him."

"No," Detroit repeated, but some of the fire had left him—like he knew the battle was already lost. "Your dad will die if he finds out you went anywhere with Wyld West."

"Your name is Wyld West? That's awesome," Micah said before flashing Detroit an irritated look. "Do you plan to tell him? What is it with my dad and you? I swear you worry way too much about his thoughts on things."

Detroit looked away, but not before Wyld caught a glimpse of what the boy was hiding. Oh, this was rich. Wyld hadn't been this entertained in a long time. He couldn't wait to enjoy this ride.

SEVEN

HENDRIX LOOKED PALE. Jude couldn't move away from his post beside him. The second they'd settled Hendrix in a room after his surgery, Jude had pulled the chair as close to the bed as possible and sat. Now, he couldn't stop toying with Hendrix's fingers beneath the blanket. Zander kept everyone updated on Hendrix's condition, freeing Jude to hover and worry. It surprised Jude, even though it shouldn't, the large number of people who'd shown up to wait for word on Hendrix. Even Wyld had arrived with some kid in tow who should definitely be turned over his daddy's knee for even thinking about hanging around Wyld. Jude couldn't worry about anyone else right now. Hendrix needed him.

While leaned over the side of the bed, Jude

rested with his cheek on his forearm next to Hendrix's head. He couldn't stop staring. His eyelids felt heavy with exhaustion and his eyeballs itched. Still, he couldn't sleep. Even though the doctor had warned him it would likely be hours before Hendrix came to, Jude didn't want Hendrix to wake up alone.

The door opened, pulling Jude's gaze away from Hendrix's sleeping face. Pytor filled the doorway. He looked unsure of his welcome.

"Is it okay if I sit with you?"

Jude had to clear his throat to make his voice work. "Of course."

Pytor filled a chair across the room and sat quietly. The man seemed content to keep Jude company in silence. Jude wasn't up to the challenge. His chest hurt, and Hendrix still had too many fucking machines hooked up to him. He wasn't okay with anything.

Jude straightened. Every bone in his back popped. He focused on Pytor. "Can I ask you about Hendrix's childhood?"

"What would you like to know?"

Jude rubbed the tips of Hendrix's fingers, trying to decide where to start. He wanted to know everything. "You said Zander raised him. What about his parents?"

Pytor cocked his head to one side and eyed Jude. A grunt escaped him that could've meant anything. "I don't know how much you know about the Conti, but Gio Conti, he was a mean bastard. His obsession with Zander was the most twisted thing I've ever seen. I don't know how he ran the West Coast with all the time he dedicated to finding ways to keep Zander under his thumb." That matched with Hendrix's insinuations, so Jude wasn't surprised. "One day, Gio showed up with Henny. The best we could guess, he was about five."

"What the fuck? You didn't even know how old he was?"

Pytor shook his head. "Gio pushed him toward Zander, and said, 'this is yours now.'"

Jude couldn't wrap his brain around Pytor's claims. Children didn't fall from the sky. Surely Hendrix had belonged to someone. "What about his parents?"

The man's giant shoulders lifted. "Gio bought Zander from his family. We assume Henny was the same. Zander gave him a name and assigned him a birthday, but Zander learned very quickly to pretend he did not care for the child. If Gio believed hurting Henny would manipulate Zander, he wouldn't hesitate." Pytor held Jude's gaze, forcing Jude to hold his breath in the face of such bleakness. "You cannot fathom the depth of Gio's cruelty. Still, Zander found ways around him. When he couldn't find ways around him, he went above and beyond to please him. In the meantime, we taught Henny to fight, because we knew he'd need it if he hoped to survive. As soon as he was old enough, Zander convinced Gio to launch Henny's fighting career, wooing him with thoughts of the boy being the youngest ever MMA champion, and making Gio lots of money. For a while, we hoped he was free."

"Then Gio told him to take a dive," Jude finished for Pytor, seeing the whole picture.

Pytor nodded. "When Gio died, I really thought he couldn't take anything else from anyone. I guess I was wrong."

Jude set his chin on his forearm and went back to staring at Hendrix. He no longer knew if the tightness in his chest was from almost losing Hendrix or hearing all his worst fears about his husband's past were true. "I've got him now."

Pytor shifted positions. The chair creaked in protest. "I know. You should get some sleep while you can."

Jude knew Pytor was right. He'd need his strength. Hendrix was counting on him.

Everything seemed far away and out of focus. Hendrix blinked several times, trying to make the room clearer. The ceiling tiles were dirty and reminded him of the gym. He squeezed his eyes shut before trying again to make his surroundings make sense. Hendrix turned his head to the right and spotted a machine. After a moment of staring at the digital numbers, he realized it showed his heart rate, oxygen, and blood pressure. The memory returned. He was in the hospital. He'd woken up several times since arriving, but the anesthesia kept pulling him back under. For the first time in who knew how long, he was finally lucid. Hendrix turned his head to the left. Jude's face was inches away. With his head resting on his arm and looking uncomfortable as fuck, he was asleep. For a moment, Hendrix stared at his gorgeous husband while trying to pull all the pieces together. He'd fucked up by trying to go back to fighting. Hendrix hadn't wanted to admit right away that he'd reinjured himself. He'd hoped after a few days of rest he'd be fine. Nothing felt fine.

He glanced down at the mountain of covers piled on his body. Hendrix knew before he flipped the blanket back what he would find. His eyes slid closed as his thoughts were confirmed. Hendrix glanced Jude's way. He slept on. The door opened and Pytor slipped inside, moving silently as always. He looked surprised to see Hendrix awake. Hendrix pressed a finger to his lips and nodded Jude's way. Considering the dark circles beneath Jude's eyes, he hadn't been sleeping. Hendrix hated to wake him yet.

"Help me," he mouthed, knowing Pytor would understand. Sometimes, being completely silent was the only way to survive living beneath the roof of a monster. They'd already done that together.

With a nod, Pytor moved to his side. Hendrix leaned on Pytor heavily as he sat up. He motioned toward the thermos of water on a rolling tray nearby. Pytor held the cup while Hendrix drank. Before Pytor could move away, Hendrix grabbed the man's wrist and lightly squeezed. It was the only sign of affection Pytor, Zander, and Yaro had ever shown each other over the years, and only when they were positive Gio wouldn't see. Pytor was as close to family as Hendrix had ever had. Hendrix loved him, but it hurt to see him. The giant guard was a reminder of things he wanted to leave behind. Not to mention, the guilt of every punishment Pytor had endured trying to protect him was massive. Hendrix didn't know how to outgrow it. With a nod, as if he read Hendrix's mind, Pytor set the cup aside before leaning in. He touched his lips to Hendrix's ear.

"I told Zander I would let him know when you were awake. Do you need anything?"

Hendrix shook his head.

Pytor pointed to the door and made a circular motion with his hand, indicating he'd be back. Hendrix nodded his understanding, and the guard was gone, leaving Hendrix alone to watch his sexy husband undisturbed.

Jude looked sexy even when he slept in the most uncomfortable looking position. Slumped over the bed with his head resting on his arm, Jude didn't budge even as Hendrix crowded his space. Because he couldn't resist, Hendrix leaned in and kissed his nose. A smile stretched his lips when Jude's nose twitched. Hendrix kissed it again. Jude's eyes opened. Hendrix's breath caught at the first sight of the sexy gray irises he'd fallen hard for.

"Good morning, gorgeous. I thought I asked you not to sleep in chairs." Even to Hendrix's ears, his voice sounded hoarse. His throat didn't feel so great.

Jude held his stare. He looked scared to move. "There's no room for me in the bed with you."

"I can scoot over."

Jude didn't smile as Hendrix hoped. "How do you feel?"

At the question, Hendrix mentally assessed his body. He hurt all over. "I've been worse." Jude's strained expression didn't clear. He felt too far away. Hendrix's heart couldn't take it. "I'm cold."

Jude's expression cleared. He sat up. "Do you need another blanket? I could get a nurse to bring you one of those heated ones."

Hendrix shook his head. "I need a hug from my bear."

Without an ounce of hesitation, Jude came to his feet. He engulfed Hendrix in his giant arms. Hendrix's eyes fell closed the second his cheek touched Jude's chest. He felt safe and loved. Jude's lips brushed Hendrix's hair. His warm breath caressed Hendrix's skin. "I love you, but—for the record—I'm so, so angry with you."

Funny. Jude didn't feel mad in Hendrix's hold. But he understood. Pytor had been there. Hendrix imagined that meant Jude knew about Zander—about him. About Gio. No one deserved to marry into that bullshit without a heads up. "I'm sorry for scaring you," Hendrix said against the man's chest, going with the apology his swollen throat would allow.

Jude's hold tightened. "I'm sorry if I did something that made you feel you had to try to kill yourself by going back to competing."

Damn. Hendrix deserved that one, and obviously Jude had learned a lot while he'd been sleeping. "I just wanted to try."

"Well, you almost died, and I don't plan to forgive you for it anytime soon."

Hendrix pushed at Jude's chest. He needed to see the man's face. Jude looked hurt. Genuinely. Guilt seeped its way in. It was like the harder he fought to be worthy of Jude, the less he became. His already sore throat swelled. He opened his mouth to apologize again, but no sound emerged. Unexpectedly, Jude went blurry. Hendrix found himself pressed against the bed, engulfed by Jude once again. It was comfort and pain rolled into one as he brushed his cheek against Jude's soft t-shirt and hunted for the sound of his heartbeat—strong and steady. Just like the man. Hendrix didn't deserve Jude. He'd known it when he'd accepted Jude's dare to marry him.

"I guess I should've paid a forfeit instead of accepting the dare to marry you," he said, sounding broken even to his ears. "At least you wouldn't have been trapped with me." The harder he fought to say the words to give Jude peace, so he could leave guilt free, the less oxygen existed in the room.

"I'm not the one who's trapped," Jude growled. Hendrix fought not to dig his fingernails into Jude's skin at the rage in the man's tone. That's how desperate he was to hang on to someone he didn't deserve—to be loved for once. Jude pulled away just enough he could meet Hendrix's stare. His fingers ran through Hendrix's hair, forcing Hendrix to fight the urge to close his eyes and savor the sensation. "You're the one who's stuck with me. Otherwise, I'll be homeless."

Hendrix blinked at the odd statement. "Why would you be homeless?"

"John has been eyeing my house for a while. You know how he likes to overcompensate." A snort escaped Hendrix at the statement. It wasn't that he didn't like John, but yeah, the house suited him. "Anyhow," Jude said, ignoring Hendrix's rude response. "I made a deal with him on it, so I could live with this really sexy younger man who was stupid enough to marry me."

"Give me his name. I'll have him killed for stealing you from me."

Jude's smile fell. He dropped his forehead to Hendrix's chest. Hendrix held the man's head while trying like hell to fight back the burning behind his eyes. He would get through this. Jude would have the best and happiest fucking husband on the planet, even if it killed Hendrix. He'd been dying inside his whole life. This was no different. He'd be damned if this touched Jude.

"I'm sorry," Jude whispered, sounding heartbroken. "The damage was too extensive. You weren't getting enough blood and oxygen to keep the tissue from dying."

Hendrix swallowed. "Well, you know what this means."

Jude lifted his chin and met Hendrix's gaze. "You won't be in pain anymore, and I will take care of you."

"That's not what I was going to say," Hendrix said with a shake of his head. "This means, I finally get to tell all the tasteless one-legged man jokes I've been saving up since childhood, and no one can call me on it."

For a moment, Jude stared at him, as if waiting to see if he'd break. Hendrix refused. He loved this man. Hendrix would be damned if he was weak and a burden. Jude shook his head. "Jesus. You're something else."

Hendrix couldn't resist stroking the bridge of

Jude's nose. "Like you said, I won't be in pain any longer. It'll be okay. I've known since the first time they tried to repair my leg that I would probably lose it if I pushed too hard." Hendrix kept stroking Jude's face, trying to comfort him. It wouldn't do for Jude to ever know the truth. They'd wanted to amputate the first time around. He'd been warned he'd spend the rest of his life in crippling pain. Gio had threatened the doctors lives if they amputated. He'd been meant to live in pain as punishment for his disobedience. This day had been nearly six years in the making. That didn't make it hurt any less. He'd never be Jude's equal.

EIGHT

AFTER FOURTEEN LONG days in the hospital, Hendrix had come home two weeks earlier with a new prosthetic and crutches until he learned to use it. Unfortunately, Hendrix hadn't really come home. He still looked the same. Sounded the same. But the man Jude went to bed with every night wasn't his Hendrix. He was a stranger.

All hours of the day, Jude fought a drowning sensation and pains in his chest. Hendrix had transformed into someone super productive but with no direction. In a span of two weeks, he'd hired people to build them a pool, so Jude wouldn't have to go without, and tore through the house, throwing away things he swore he didn't need. Hendrix claimed he wanted Jude to have space for his things and feel at home, but it all felt manic. His mother was bipolar, and Jude recognized the desperation in Hendrix's eyes. The driving need to not stop. Get things done. Keep life moving so the pain wouldn't catch up. It was terrifying.

Jude fought for any way to reach him. "I'm headed out to run some errands. Come with me."

Hendrix flashed him an overly bright smile. "No thanks. Oh, but hey, pick up some marshmallows while you're out, please."

Jude didn't want to push, but Hendrix never left the house for anything but doctors' visits. "Are you sure? I plan to stop by the gym and pay your dues while I'm out."

"Of course, I'm sure. I need marshmallows to make those crispy cereal treat thingies."

Avoidance. Again. Jude had hoped stopping by the gym would lure Hendrix out. The man had tons of people there who were—no doubt—itching to see him, but he refused to budge. Jude let it drop. "What's got you in here cooking? I don't think I've ever actually seen that."

Hendrix waved a wooden spoon around. "I don't cook, but I'm thinking I'll teach myself. It'll give me something to do, and I've been craving some ridiculous things lately. Hence the marshmallows."

Jude crossed the room and invaded Hendrix's space. "I'm not sure those count as cooking, since you can make those in the microwave," Jude said as he molded against Hendrix's back and peeked over his shoulder at the cookbook he had open on the counter.

Hendrix glanced over, looking crestfallen. "You can?"

Jude fought the urge to scream. It was like he was watching Hendrix drown and scramble for anything to keep him sane. Yet, Hendrix still put on a strong face. Jude didn't know if it was for him or if Hendrix didn't know how to be any other way. He kept Zander's advice at the forefront of his mind at all times. If he planned to spend his life with this man who'd endured things he'd never understand, he needed to learn to deal with things he'd never understand. For a fixer like him, it wasn't easy.

He kissed Hendrix's neck. "I love you. I'll grab a couple of bags and we can make them together. They taste better when cooked on the stove anyhow."

Hendrix held the back of Jude's head, urging his lips back to his neck. He heard Hendrix's breath catch as he brushed kisses along Hendrix's throat. His cock stirred at the sound. He took a step back.

The last thing Hendrix needed was Jude pawing at him.

"I'll be back in a few. Are you sure you don't want to go?"

Hendrix still smiled, but a hint of sadness tinted his features. "I'm sure." Jude took a step toward the door. Hendrix reached out and snagged his shirt, pulling the material tight against Jude's skin. "Hey."

Jude glanced over.

Hendrix looked real for the first time since coming home. "I love you too." He released Jude's shirt, and the moment was over as quickly as it began, but Jude's throat burned. He wanted his husband back. Sometimes, he worried Hendrix would never go back to being the man who'd spent two weeks with him on that boat. Jude would find him again. He pressed a quick kiss to Hendrix's lips.

"I'll be fast," Jude promised, heading for the door. He couldn't fix things if he wasn't here.

By the time he made it to Powerhouse Training, Jude was itching to get back home. He hated letting Hendrix out of his sight. All he could think about was what if something happened while he was gone? Hendrix was still adjusting. Fuck. He needed to get his errands run and get home. Once inside, Jude tried to hurry, but people kept stopping him to ask about Hendrix. He almost made it back out the door when someone else stepped into his path. Jude considered barreling past them until he realized it was Zander. Considering how the man was dressed —in an expensive suit, Jude assumed he was only there to be with Maverick.

"How's Hendrix?"

Jude opened his mouth to give the same "he's good" speech he'd given everyone else. It didn't come. "Fuck if I know." Once the first confession fell, Jude couldn't stop. He rubbed his forehead, hoping he didn't look as torn to pieces as he felt. "I mean, he smiles a lot—like seriously, a lot. But it's fake, you know? I'm not sure if I should shake him or pretend like I don't notice, so I do nothing. If I try talking to him, he evades."

Zander winced. "Sorry. I taught him that one. For survival purposes," he added unnecessarily. "If someone asks about your life, change the subject. If they won't relent, tell them an equally important secret to force them off topic. If you do both those things and they still keep talking, flirt."

Jude opened his mouth to respond before snapping his teeth together. Fuck. How many times had he fallen for that? Asking about Hendrix's childhood had gotten him information on the man's leg, and a few blow jobs. "Damn." The thought of blow jobs had Jude fighting back a blush. Zander had raised Hendrix. He was like the man's father. "Um, about the restaurant."

Zander threw his head back and roared with laughter. Several heads turned their way. Jude's embarrassment slipped away. Happiness transformed Zander into someone else—someone human. Zander swiped at his eyes. "Yeah, that was a surprise." He swiped at his eyes again, obviously still fighting back his laughter. Once he had himself under control, Zander focused on him once more. "Listen, I came from the same hell as Hendrix, so I don't have any advice. All I can do is tell you what Maverick does for me."

Jude didn't hesitate. "I'll take it."

Zander's expression screamed understanding. "He loves me. Every day, with tiny ridiculous acts of kindness that overwhelm me because I've never had that in my life before him. If Hendrix is doing something out of the ordinary to make it through another day, embrace it. Make it fun. Go along with him. Just be there when it happens so he'll know you'll be there when it passes. Or, you can force him to talk." Zander held his stare. Jude hung on every word. "It's okay to get mad as long as you don't leave.

You can lose your temper if you can't get through to him. It won't break him. Just don't leave, because that will probably kill him, and then I'll kill you."

Despite knowing Zander was one hundred percent serious, Jude wasn't bothered. "He'll have to kill me himself if he wants me gone."

At the confession, Zander gave him a sharp nod. His hardened expression transformed, and his gaze skirted away. For the first time, Zander looked uncomfortable. "I've been trying to text him, but he keeps ignoring me."

"I'll talk to him," Jude said without thought.

Zander shook his head. "It won't make a difference. We're too far gone, but maybe—if you don't mind—you could keep me posted." Zander winced as if he expected to get shot down.

"No problem. He has a doctor's appointment next week. I'll text you afterward."

The way Zander's features didn't relax said a lot about how much he hated asking for anything. "Thank you." His gaze slid toward the cage where Maverick sparred with some guy Jude didn't recognize. Zander never looked away from Maverick as he spoke. "Thank you for more than keeping me posted. If I could've picked anyone for Henny, it would've been you. He deserves someone who loves him the way you do." His gaze finally slid back Jude's way. "Someone strong enough to handle him."

Jude only managed a nod. Words failed him. In truth, he didn't feel strong at the moment. He didn't know if he had what he needed to help Hendrix, but he wouldn't give up. Right now, all he could do was buy marshmallows and hope for the best.

———

HENDRIX HAD NO CONCEPT OF TIME AS IT passed. He stared out the back window at the construction equipment parked in his backyard. Soon, they'd have a new pool. No matter how hard Hendrix tried to care, he couldn't. The only thing inside his head was the way Jude had backed away after kissing his neck. He'd never experienced pain like the sting of Jude's rejection. Since losing the use of his leg, no one had looked at him like he was sexy until Jude. Not only did Jude look at him like he'd never met anyone hotter, he'd been falling on Hendrix like he couldn't get enough from the first night. Not anymore. When they'd amputated Hendrix's leg just below the knee, he'd lost more than a limb. Hendrix had lost Jude's desire. It was worse than dying. In fact, it would've been better if

Jude had let him die, rather than keeping him around for the sake of pity. He needed to set the man free.

The familiar jingle of Jude's cellphone cut through Hendrix's thoughts. His gaze shot around the room before landing on the device. Realizing Jude must've set it down before leaving and forgotten it, Hendrix retrieved it. He didn't recognize the number, but the area code was local. Hendrix chewed his bottom lip. He didn't want to answer Jude's phone. It seemed wrong somehow. The ringing stopped, saving him from having to choose. Before he could put the phone back where he found it, it started back again. Same number. What if it was Jude, trying to find his phone? Fuck it. He answered.

"Hello?"

"Who is this?" The woman's accusing tone almost made Hendrix hang up.

Instead, he stuck with it. "Hendrix. Jude's husband. He forgot his ph—"

"Good," she said, cutting him off. "It's you I wanted to talk to. Well, first I intended to give Jude an earful, but then I wanted to talk to you."

"Okay," Hendrix said dragging out the word.

She didn't slow. "Do you know how I found out my son had gotten married?" This was Jude's mom? Fuck. Hendrix didn't have a family. He hadn't considered Jude not calling his. She didn't wait for Hendrix to think of a response. "Fourth fucking hand, that's how. I ran into a friend who'd seen another friend who knew someone that knew someone who'd heard about it. Can you believe that?"

Hendrix winced. "That's probably my fault."

Her voice transformed, turning sweet. "I heard about your surgery too. That's not your fault, sweetie."

Hendrix's chin hit his chest. His vision blurred. He didn't know how this woman he'd never met hit him so hard with her comfort, saying exactly what he needed to hear, but there didn't seem to be enough oxygen in the room any longer. He drew a ragged breath. "Thank you. I can't believe he didn't call you. If I'd known, I would've nagged him nonstop."

A wicked-sounding chuckle came through the phone. "I'm Viv, by the way."

"It's nice to meet you, Viv."

"You too, Hendrix. I'm ridiculously excited to have a new son." The claim punched Hendrix so hard in the chest, he caught himself rubbing his sternum. He spent the next fifteen minutes, listening to how Viv would never have grandkids and how she loved to tell her boys how they disappointed her even though everyone involved knew it was a joke. She couldn't be prouder of the boys she'd raised. Her love was in her voice for anyone to hear. Hendrix let the minutes wash over him, bringing him a modicum of peace. By the time they said their goodbyes, he felt a lot better.

Then, his gaze landed on the disarray that was their unfinished pool again. Crippling fear slammed into him. What if everything ended right here? What if Jude decided he didn't want the mess that was Hendrix? He hadn't known who he was marrying when he'd dared Hendrix to marry him. Jude hadn't known Hendrix had been raised at the feet of the throne of Hell. He hadn't realized that Hendrix was broken inside beyond repair. Now Jude knew, and it was possible he was done. Hendrix couldn't breathe at the thought.

Jude filled the doorway, carrying several grocery bags. "I refuse to make more than one trip," he said with a laugh as he dumped the bags on the floor. The light gray stare Hendrix loved focused on him. "Oh, good. You found my phone," he said, relieving Hendrix of the device and shoving it in his back pocket. "I searched my SUV for ten minutes, thinking it had fallen out of my pocket."

Hendrix had forgotten he'd been holding it. "I

had a moment of stupidity where I almost texted you to tell you that you'd forgotten your phone," Hendrix joked, because he'd forgotten how to be real with anyone so damn long ago he didn't know how to do so now. Even if it meant saving himself, he couldn't beg for a lifeline. Hendrix eyed the bags. "What's all this?"

Jude's bright smile never wavered. It looked as fake as Hendrix's felt. "You said you wanted to learn to cook. I thought we'd make dinner together. Something unhealthy, because your dessert choice has my inner fat kid happy dancing."

Hendrix stared at Jude's profile as he unpacked the bags. He didn't bother looking to see what food items Jude had bought. Words and confessions rose in Hendrix's throat, choking him, but he didn't know where to start. He wanted to beg Jude to stay with him. To look at him the way he had their first night together. His lips refused to work.

Jude found a pot and filled it with water. "I saw Zander today, and it got me to thinking. Maybe we should go see them. Pytor sat with you a lot at the hospital. It's obvious they care."

Hendrix focused on his hands, clinging to the edge of the counter. His knuckles were white. "I forgot to tell you, I found a bunch of new one-legged man jokes online yesterday."

"Don't do that."

Even Jude's quietly spoken plea couldn't force Hendrix's lips to stop moving. "Also, your mom called. She had a lot to say about finding out—fourth-hand, I believe she called it—that we're married."

"That's the least of the ways I've disappointed her. Please stop."

Jude's dead tone set warning bells clanging in Hendrix's head, but it was too late. A laugh that sounded fake even to him escaped Hendrix. "Don't worry. I told her about John's arrangement with the two barely eighteen-year-olds and she forgot all about missing our wedding."

The pot of water in Jude's hand flew across the room, crashing against the wall before slamming to the floor. Hendrix stared at it in disbelief. He tore his gaze away from the mess and focused on Jude. Jude's shoulders heaved, but he didn't move. He stared straight ahead as if the window above the sink was the only thing keeping him from tearing into a rage.

When Jude spoke, his voice came out low and deadly, as if he measured each word to keep from screaming. "I need you to let me in, Hendrix. If you can't do that, I don't know how to make us work."

Hendrix licked his rapidly drying lips. He hated this. "What do you mean?"

Jude still didn't look his way. "Every time I ask you about anything the least bit personal, or talk about Zander, you change the subject or crack a joke." He turned his head and met Hendrix's stare. "You shut Zander out, and I get it, but now you're shutting me out too. I don't how much longer I can stand it."

Hendrix couldn't lose Jude. The idea of Jude walking away was the only thing that unglued his tongue from the roof of his mouth. "You don't understand." Even Hendrix heard the desperation in his voice. "Whatever hell you're imagining my life was growing up, it was twenty times worse than that. Now, whatever hell you're picturing with that newfound knowledge, Zander's life was two million times worse than that. I have to live with knowing it was because he chose to keep me safe every day. It's not that I'm trying to shut you out. I'm trying to hang onto my sanity by keeping that shut in." Hendrix stared at Jude, silently pleading for him to understand. "A new life started for me when I met you. One where I felt whole and safe. I've never had that." He looked away. It hurt too much to see Jude's disappointment. "I'm not surprised I failed you right away, because no one gave me the tools I need to be who you want. But please know, I've always just wanted to be worthy of you." Every word hurt like glass in his throat because he knew in his heart Jude was already gone. The man had been gone five minutes after Hendrix had been released from the hospital. Jude might've stayed with him physically, but he'd already filed for divorce in his heart. Hendrix focused on the mess on the floor because he couldn't watch Jude go. "I'm sorry I didn't turn out to be who you wanted. If you ever need anything, find Zander. He'll make sure you're taken care of."

"What if what I need is you?"

Hendrix's gaze refused to budge from the wall. No one would ever know how fucking exhausted he was. "You won't." No one needed that, especially not someone as amazing as Jude.

Jude invaded Hendrix's space. "Answer me," Jude demanded, snagging Hendrix's jaw and forcing him to meet the beautiful gray stare he'd fallen in love with. "What if what I need is you?"

Jude blurred. Hendrix's eyes burned. His throat swelled. "No one needs that."

"I do, goddamn it," Jude snapped, slamming his fist down on the counter next to Hendrix, making Hendrix jump. He poked himself in the chest. "I do.

If you don't ever want to see Zander again, that's up to you. I'm not asking you to drag up the past. I'm asking you to stop fucking pretending like you're fine. If you're upset or angry, say it. Break something. Hate fuck me. I can take it. For the love of god, please stop trying to second guess what I want. I. Want. You. From the first fucking day, I've never been anything other than straight with you. I'll be damned if I start sugarcoating shit now. You're mine —fucked up. Pissed off. Broken inside. All that— mine." Jude punctuated his growled words by slamming his fist down on the counter once more.

A sad smile tugged at Hendrix's lips at Jude's show of temper. "Bear."

Jude's shoulders fell at Hendrix's name calling— like the fire bled from him. He dropped his forehead to Hendrix's shoulder. Hendrix couldn't resist wrapping his arms around Jude's waist. Jude turned his head and pressed his lips to the side of Hendrix's neck. He stayed like that. His hot breath fanned across Hendrix's skin. "Pup," he said against Hendrix's throat.

Hendrix swallowed. The burning was back behind his eyes. His fingers curled around Jude's shirt, holding the man in place. It was out of his control. There was no pride when it came to Jude. "I love you. Please don't go. I'm scared." He felt Jude's chest expand before a ragged-sounding breath escaped him.

"I'm scared too." Jude's confession surprised Hendrix enough he leaned back, needing to see Jude's face. He never would've expected Jude to say such a thing. Jude didn't look away. "I'm petrified that I'll come home one day, and you'll be gone or dead. Every day, I see you silently suffering and trying to hide it. I've never felt more helpless." He cupped Hendrix's face. "I would never leave you. Please stop trying to leave me."

Hendrix blinked, trying to bring Jude in focus. "I'm terrified that you'll never stop looking at me like you are now—like I'm broken. It scares the shit out of me that you'll keep pulling away from me every time I kiss you, and I'll never get to feel equal again." Jude hadn't blinked since Hendrix started talking. Hendrix wasn't sure he was breathing, but the confessions were falling, and he couldn't stop. "Before losing my leg, you were the only person who treated me like I'm whole. I know I'm not. I never have been, but you made me feel like I could be." Hendrix swallowed. He really didn't want to cry. Everything hurt. "Now, I look on the outside how I've always been on the inside, missing pieces. You see it now, and I don't know how much longer I can take it. I don't know how many more times I can stand you kissing me and turning away just as fast— like you don't want me anymore." Hendrix choked on the last word. He'd been unwanted before Jude, but losing Jude's passion for him was so much worse.

Jude finally blinked. He visibly swallowed, as if his throat hurt. When he spoke, he sounded hoarse. "You think I don't want you anymore?"

Hendrix glanced away. "It's okay. You didn't sign up for a mess."

Jude cupped Hendrix's jaw and held him in place, leaving Hendrix no choice but to look at him. "You seriously think I don't want you anymore?"

Hendrix thought about the way Jude had backed away from their kiss earlier. A pain sliced through him. It showed in his voice. "Yes."

The final inch between them disappeared. Hendrix found himself trapped between the counter and Jude's large body. There was so much heat in Jude's eyes, Hendrix's mouth went dry at the sight. There was no missing the way Jude went hard. Jude couldn't fake that reaction. To Hendrix's surprise, he found himself lifted from the ground and his ass on the edge of the counter, leaving Hendrix no other choice but to cling to the man's large shoulders.

Jude's large frame filled the space between his knees. "Baby, I've just been waiting for you to give me the green light. Not having you has been killing me. I didn't want to hurt you accidentally."

Hendrix had always thought sex was an insignificant thing until he thought Jude didn't want to touch him. Now, he thought he'd die without that connection to this man who'd completely stolen him. "I miss your mouth on my skin."

The final word hadn't died on Hendrix's lips before he found himself over Jude's shoulder and headed for the bedroom.

WHILE JUDE REALIZED THEY WERE NEW AT THIS being married business, and their start had been interrupted by tragedy, they were so fucking stupid. Jude had spent so much time thinking Hendrix was mourning his loss, and trying to be considerate of that, it never occurred to him that his consideration was the problem. From the very beginning, Hendrix had shown him that he needed someone bold. Yet, Jude had been anything but, since finding out about the man's past. That shit was over. Hendrix had given him a peek inside. Jude had seen who he needed to be. Lucky him, because Hendrix required a man who would make him feel as sexy as he was. Jude had this. No complaints.

It had been the longest month of his life not being inside Hendrix, which was funny because he'd gone months without sex before. There were dry spells, and then there was knowing what he was missing with Hendrix. The two situations were nothing alike. He was careful with Hendrix on the way to the bedroom in all the ways he needed to be since Hendrix was still sore. But he had no intentions of being gentle in any other way.

Jude set Hendrix on the bed. "Strip." The growl Hendrix always accused him of having was out of his control when it came to his sexy husband. There was so much desire and possessiveness inside him when it came to Hendrix, Jude didn't know where to go with it. "I like to watch." Damn, he really did.

A blush bloomed on Hendrix's cheeks, fascinating Jude. Hendrix had never been embarrassed or shy with him before. Jude pulled his shirt off, hoping his nudity would get Hendrix started. As his fingers went for the button of his jeans, Hendrix pulled his shirt up and over his head. Jude's mouth went dry.

"Keep going," Jude urged as he unzipped his

pants. While Hendrix tugged off the rest of his clothes, Jude stripped and palmed his cock. He was so turned on already, he didn't think he'd last long.

Once nude, Hendrix fell back against the mattress, waiting, and looking exactly like a man about to get fucked. Hendrix licked his lips. "What now?"

Jude moved to the bedside table, suited up, and coated his dick in lube before meeting Hendrix's stare again. He wanted Hendrix to feel the same desperate longing. "Ass to the edge of the bed."

Hendrix immediately complied.

Jude hauled the lower half of Hendrix's body higher and probed at the man's asshole with his cock without any prep. Hendrix needed this. It wasn't time to make love, even though that's always what it was for Jude. He ground his back teeth as Hendrix's body gave, accepting him inside. Tight heat squeezed his dick. Hendrix's expression had Jude fighting back his orgasm. No one made him hot like Hendrix. Once fully seated, Jude held Hendrix's injured leg close to his body, keeping it still, and ensuring he wouldn't get hurt. Once he was certain Hendrix would feel nothing but pleasure, Jude rocked inside Hendrix, hitting all the right spots, before pulling almost all the way out and slamming back inside again.

Hendrix sucked in a gasp. His eyes fell closed, and he visibly swallowed before sucking air. It was the sexiest sight Jude had ever seen. He couldn't go another second without tasting Hendrix's lips. Jude urged him higher on the bed before settling between the man's thighs and opening his mouth over Hendrix's. Their tongues clashed, stroking as if fighting to get closer as Jude rocked inside Hendrix. Jude tore his mouth away and placed open mouthed kisses along Hendrix's jaw. He nipped at the man's skin.

"Goddamn, Hendrix. How could you ever think I don't want this? You're so fucking perfect."

Hendrix pushed against him, taking his pleasure. The sounds he made drove Jude insane. "Love you," Hendrix gasped out between moans. "Scared as fuck to lose you."

Jude's motions slowed. He sucked at Hendrix's throat. "Not possible," he whispered against Hendrix's skin. "I can't give up every memory we haven't made yet. We have to spend more time on the water, letting the water rock us as I make love to you. I want you to sit in my lap and watch the sunset. It would kill me if I thought I'd never get to hear you laugh again." A wave of pleasure stole Jude's breath. "I'm so fucking in love with you," Jude whispered against Hendrix's throat. "Play with yourself, baby. I don't know how much longer I can hold out."

Hendrix reached between them and stroked his cock.

Jude's lust skyrocketed. "Fuck, Hendrix. You're not leaving this bed anytime soon." A mixture of pleasure and pressure threatened to tear him apart. "Goddamn. Not going to make it. You feel too fucking amazing." Jude's balls drew up tight. He couldn't slow. Every thrust was hard and deep. Jude pressed his forehead to Hendrix's shoulder, squeezed his eyes shut, and raced toward the edge. The way Hendrix moaned—like he'd never felt anything better than Jude's dick inside him, sent Jude flying into a blinding orgasm. Even once it hit, he couldn't stop rocking against Hendrix, hoping to make it last forever. Cum coated his stomach, letting him know Hendrix must've come. He'd been so engrossed in the way Hendrix blew him away that he couldn't focus on anything other than his pleasure.

Time ticked by without a care from Jude as he savored Hendrix's mouth. He never got enough of tasting Hendrix's lips and tongue. At some point, he moved away only long enough to clean up their mess, but then he was back. The sensation of Hendrix in his arms, where he fit perfectly, was the best fucking feeling in the world. He finally felt like they'd be okay for the first time in what felt like forever. The harder he tried to stop kissing and stroking Hendrix, the more the need rose in his chest to continue.

He rolled Hendrix onto his stomach, worried the man's back and sexy ass felt neglected of kisses. When he reached the sexy indentations above Hendrix's ass, his cellphone rang, dragging a loud sigh from him. Fuck. All he wanted was this. Why hadn't he turned his phone off? Jude hunted through his clothes at the edge of the bed, searching for his phone. He groaned when he caught sight of his mom's number. She'd already called and talked to Hendrix earlier in the day. If he ignored her now, she might show up at their door, and he wasn't finished with Hendrix yet.

"It's Mom," he warned before answering. "Hello?"

"I'm mad at you. Put Hendrix on the phone."

A short laugh burst from his throat. "Okay, then." He passed the phone to Hendrix. "She wants to talk to you."

The way Hendrix smiled fascinated Jude.

Hendrix looked happy to talk to his mom and pressed the phone to his ear. "Hey, Viv."

"Viv?" Jude mouthed behind him. No one called his mom Viv but her best friend. With a shake of his head, Jude went back to kissing Hendrix's nape and between his shoulder blades. He loved the way Hendrix's warm skin felt against his lips. With one ear locked on Hendrix's side of the conversation, Jude lightly sank his teeth into every new inch of bared skin.

"That sounds good to me. Thank you. That's so thoughtful." Hendrix moved the phone away from his mouth and sucked in a breath when Jude caressed his hip. Jude bit back a chuckle. "No. My parents are both dead." Jude froze with his lips still pressed to Hendrix's spine at the words. "My mom passed away when I was five, and my father passed a few years back." Jude hung on every word. He didn't know if Hendrix was simply bullshitting his mom to keep her happy or if Hendrix actually knew who his parents were. "I do have extended family you could invite though." Jude sat up and openly stared at Hendrix. "Zander, Pytor, and Yaro. I'll text you the address later." Hendrix brought Jude's hand to his mouth and kissed his palm. "Don't worry over it. I'll make sure Jude is there. If you want, I'll hold him, and you can spank him." Jude rolled his eyes. He could hear his mother laughing through the phone. "I'll talk to you later. Hugs back." Hendrix handed the phone back. "She's throwing a wedding reception for us."

Jude swallowed down a groan as he set the phone aside. He didn't want Hendrix to think he was unhappy, but he fucking hated parties. Of course, it was a party celebrating his love for Hendrix, and he would be there.

Hendrix rolled onto his back. He looked unsure of himself. "I hope your people like me."

"They're your people now too," Jude reminded him. He straddled Hendrix's hips, keeping his weight balanced on his knees to keep from squishing Hendrix. "Besides, it doesn't really matter if they like you, because I love you, and—apparently so does my mom."

"She's nice," Hendrix said with a shrug.

Having such a sexy man pinned beneath him was tempting as hell, but Jude couldn't let the moment pass. "Was all that true? About your parents? Pytor said they never knew who your parents were."

Hendrix nodded. "I might've been five when I came to live with them, but I remember my mom.

Well, parts of her," Hendrix admitted. "She had long, curly red hair. I liked to sit on her lap and play with her hair. She always smelled like candy." Jude couldn't look away. He was afraid if he moved a muscle, Hendrix would lock down again, refusing to let him in. "I remember being at the funeral home, seeing her sleeping in a wooden box, and screaming because she wouldn't wake up. An older lady kept telling me to calm down, and that my dad would be there soon to take me to live in a castle."

A realization hit Jude with enough force, it nearly stole his breath. "So, Gio was your real father?"

Something dark passed over Hendrix's features and Jude wished he could take it away. Hendrix nodded, confirming Jude's fears. "No one knows that. Not even Zander. I don't want him ever to know. Hell, I wish I didn't know. After I moved out on my own, I started digging, trying quietly to find my family. I figured, even if they sold me to Gio the way Zander's family had, that it couldn't hurt to know who they were. Plus, I had that memory of my mom, you know. It took some time, but I finally found a friend of my mom's family who knew the story." Hendrix shrugged. His gaze stayed locked on Jude's chest, obviously struggling to pretend it didn't matter. "In Gio's world, you were whoever he told you to be. I believe he thought he could give me to Zander and turn Zander into the same monster he was." Hendrix's chest expanded as he took a deep breath before meeting Jude's gaze. His eyes were so dead that Jude would've asked him to stop if he could've made his tongue work. "You have no idea what Zander endured for me. There's only been one time I've ever been able to hold his stare. When I tried to kill him."

There was nothing Hendrix could say that would ever make him run away. Jude made sure his tone showed that. "Obviously, you didn't scare him away. That's something."

Hendrix's mouth lifted in one corner. "If that doesn't tell you how fucked up we are then nothing will."

Jude went down onto his elbows, going nose to nose with Hendrix. He smattered light kisses along the bridge of his nose before moving to do the same to his cheekbones. "I don't see a messed-up man here. All I see is the man I love, waiting to keep me happy. Jesus. Tell me again how I got so lucky?"

Hendrix's hands ran up his back, stealing Jude's heart with his gentle touch, the way he always did. He sounded breathless when he spoke. "I limped my way down a really long hallway just to sit next to you. There were other people sitting alone that night, but I just kept walking." Hendrix's hold tightened on Jude. "Then I spotted you. It was like you were sitting there waiting for me."

At the confession, Jude leaned away. His gaze moved over Hendrix's face. It hadn't occurred to him before now, but Hendrix had walked a long way for a seat that night. He was right. The night they'd come together had felt like fate—like he'd been waiting for Hendrix's arrival. Now he had the husband of his dreams. Jude didn't ever intend to let anything come between them. Not Hendrix's past or his own insecurities. "Let's make a deal to always talk to each other from now on instead of trying to fix shit with zero clue what we're fixing. Because, for real Hendrix, I don't ever want to lose you. I think I was only half of me before you, and I'll be even less if you're gone."

Jude heard Hendrix swallow. His voice came out sounding hoarse when he responded, "Agreed."

With Hendrix's agreement in place, Jude went back trying to steal all his pup's kisses. They would rock at this marriage thing. Flying by the seat of their pants and doing things in reverse was their specialty. They were fucking perfect.

NINE

THE WEDDING RECEPTION Viv threw together was beautiful and packed with people Hendrix didn't know. Thankfully, Zander, Yaro, and Pytor had shown so Hendrix's side wasn't completely unrepresented. There were a few other familiar faces in the crowd, but mostly it was Viv's friends. The moment they'd arrived, Hendrix had found his face pressed against John's massive chest... again. As much as Hendrix hated to admit it, the guy was growing on him. John only had Jonah with him. Hendrix fought the urge to pepper Jude with questions over that one. Instead, he stayed glued to Jude's side in the backyard of Viv's beachside cottage —as close to the open bar as he could get. Walking on crutches in the sand would've been a complete nightmare if Viv hadn't set up special walkways. Three hours in, Hendrix loved Jude's mom like she was his own, and he still wasn't drunk enough to relax in the crowd.

Detroit appeared out of nowhere, looking like the world's sexiest player, as always. "What's Wyld doing here?" he asked, reaching between Hendrix and Jude to grab a beer.

Hendrix shrugged, finding Wyld in the crowd with his gaze. "Jude's mom is friends with someone who knows someone that invited him. He's not so bad once you get to know him."

Detroit stared at him like he'd lost his mind. "Are you joking?"

Jude nodded toward where Wyld had the young guy who'd come to the reception with Detroit cornered. "Your friend seems to like him."

Detroit turned so fast, Hendrix didn't know how he stayed upright. "Fuck," he muttered under his breath.

Hendrix bit back a laugh at the curse. He couldn't imagine anyone liking Wyld better than Detroit. But from where he stood, it looked like he was seeing it now.

"Micah likes everyone," Detroit muttered, sounding aggravated. "It's a wonder he hasn't turned up dead in a ditch."

Hendrix fought the urge to point out how Detroit sounded like the guy's dad rather than his friend. Before he could think of anything to say, Detroit released a loud sigh. "I suppose I'd better go save him. Congrats on the marriage, guys. It's great to see you both so happy."

Jude tucked Hendrix tighter against his side as Detroit walked away. He touched his lips to the shell of Hendrix's ear, bringing goosebumps to his skin. "You have been smiling a lot lately, pup. I wonder why that is."

Hendrix had to take a breath. Being married to Jude was so much of everything amazing, he didn't know how to stop smiling. Once he'd let go and embraced that Jude really did love him, ugly past and all, everything had fallen into place.

"It's because I married this super sexy b—"

"Congrats," Wyld said, interrupting Hendrix.

Hendrix pasted on a smile. Damn, he really wanted to find a quiet spot to molest his husband. "Thank you." His gaze slid to the boy flanking Wyld. He held out his hand. "I'm Hendrix."

"Micah," the blond said, accepting his hand shake.

"The angel of miracles," Wyld added as he tossed back a shot of whisky.

Hendrix ignored Wyld. He didn't release Micah right away. "Nice to meet you Micah. You should probably get away from this one as fast as possible."

To his surprise, Wyld nodded his agreement and Micah's smile brightened. "I know, but we're friends. I've always had a soft spot for the criminally conceited."

His description surprised a bark of laughter from Hendrix.

"Did someone say my name?" Detroit said, slinging his arm over Micah's shoulders. "Hey, cutie. Let's find you something to eat."

Micah flashed them an uncomfortable smile as Detroit steered him away.

Wyld rolled his eyes but didn't watch them go.

Hendrix couldn't tear his gaze away from Wyld. Sometimes, he got the feeling there was a human buried somewhere deep, deep inside the spoiled tycoon.

Wyld focused on him. A light entered his eyes that gave Hendrix a bad feeling in his gut. "Hear me out," he said, making Hendrix stifle a groan. "Special Olympics."

Hendrix's groan refused to be suppressed twice. "No. I'm not listening to this."

"Come on," Wyld cajoled. "There's nothing holding you back now. You're still in fighting shape. I've got nothing but time and money to throw your way. Let's do this."

Hendrix glanced Jude's way, looking for some backup. Instead, Jude appeared thoughtful. "No," Hendrix repeated, but no one listened.

"You could do it."

Hendrix's mind went blank at Jude's quietly spoken words. It was obvious both men were serious. A kernel of hope burst to life. Hendrix wanted to stamp it down. His gaze moved between Wyld and Jude. They stared back, looking expectant. "I'll think about it."

Wyld pumped a fist in the air. Hendrix ignored him. He couldn't stop staring at the smile stretching Jude's lips. Jude was proud to be married to him. It was evident in the man's every word and deed. As Hendrix stared at Jude, he made a silent vow. For the rest of his life, he'd be worthy of Jude. This gorgeous bear would never regret him. He might take Wyld's offer or he might dedicate his time to something else. Either way, Jude would always come first.

"Run away with me." The offer was out there before Hendrix realized he would say it. He couldn't stop. "I dare you to disappear with me."

The smile that lit Jude's face let him know he wouldn't have to come up with a forfeit. Jude focused on Wyld. "Cover for us, and I'll make sure Hendrix shows up to start training the moment his doctor feels he's ready."

"Done," Wyld said, not hesitating to conspire against Hendrix.

Hendrix could only blink as he watched his life being planned for him. As Jude swept him through a back gate, Hendrix marveled over how much his life had changed in such a short amount of time. It looked like things would be changing even more soon. He would go along for the ride. Jude had never steered him wrong before now. They would have a happy life. Hendrix felt it in his gut.

PLEASE CONSIDER LEAVING A REVIEW AT THE retailer where this book was purchased. Reviews really help with a book's visibility, which ensures I can continue writing. Thank you, Charity.

KEEP AN EYE OUT FOR THE NEXT BOOK IN THE Sugar Daddies series, Sugar Tycoon.

ABOUT THE AUTHOR

Charity Parkerson is an award winning and multi-published author with several companies. Born with no filter from her brain to her mouth, she decided to take this odd quirk and insert it in her characters.

*Seven-time Readers' Favorite Award Winner
  *2015 Passionate Plume Award Finalist
  *2013 Reviewers' Choice Award Winner
  *2012 ARRA Finalist for Favorite Paranormal Romance
  *Five-time winner of The Mistress of the Darkpath

Connect with her online:

--Join my street team: facebook.com/TeamCharityParkerson
  --Sign up for my newsletter: http://bit.ly/CharityNews
  --Website: charityparkerson.com

--Facebook:
facebook.com/authorCharityParkerson
facebook.com/TheMenofSin
--Twitter: twitter.com/CharityParkerso